G R JORDAN

Boomtown

A Highlands and Islands Detective Thriller Book 35

Carpetless

First published by Carpetless Publishing 2024

First edition

ISBN: 978-1-915562-97-5

This book was professionally typeset on Reedsy.
Find out more at reedsy.com

When all else fails: explosions.

Laini Taylor

Contents

Foreword

The events of this book, while based around real and also fictitious locations around Scotland, are entirely fictional and all characters do not represent any living or deceased person. All companies are fictitious representations. This book was produced against a ticking clock.

Acknowledgement

To Ken, Jean, Colin, Evelyn, John and Rosemary for your work in bringing this novel to completion, your time and effort is deeply appreciated.

Books by G R Jordan

The Highlands and Islands Detective series (Crime)

1. Water's Edge
2. The Bothy
3. The Horror Weekend
4. The Small Ferry
5. Dead at Third Man
6. The Pirate Club
7. A Personal Agenda
8. A Just Punishment
9. The Numerous Deaths of Santa Claus
10. Our Gated Community
11. The Satchel
12. Culhwch Alpha
13. Fair Market Value
14. The Coach Bomber
15. The Culling at Singing Sands
16. Where Justice Fails
17. The Cortado Club
18. Cleared to Die
19. Man Overboard!
20. Antisocial Behaviour
21. Rogues' Gallery
22. The Death of Macleod - Inferno Book 1

23. A Common Man - Inferno Book 2
24. A Sweeping Darkness - Inferno Book 3
25. Dormie 5
26. The First Minister - Past Mistakes Book 1
27. The Guilty Parties - Past Mistakes Book 2
28. Vengeance is Mine - Past Mistakes Book 3
29. Winter Slay Bells
30. Macleod's Cruise
31. Scrambled Eggs
32. The Esoteric Tear
33. A Rock 'n' Roll Murder
34. The Slaughterhouse
35. Boomtown
36. The Absent Sculptor
37. A Trip to Rome
38. A Time to Rest
39. Cinderella's Carriage
40. Wild Swimming

Kirsten Stewart Thrillers (Thriller)

1. A Shot at Democracy
2. The Hunted Child
3. The Express Wishes of Mr MacIver
4. The Nationalist Express
5. The Hunt for 'Red Anna'
6. The Execution of Celebrity
7. The Man Everyone Wanted
8. Busman's Holiday

9. A Personal Favour
10. Infiltrator
11. Implosion
12. Traitor

Jac Moonshine Thrillers

1. Jac's Revenge
2. Jac for the People
3. Jac the Pariah

Siobhan Duffy Mysteries

1. A Giant Killing
2. Death of the Witch
3. The Bloodied Hands
4. A Hermit's Death

The Contessa Munroe Mysteries (Cozy Mystery)

1. Corpse Reviver
2. Frostbite
3. Cobra's Fang

The Patrick Smythe Series (Crime)

1. The Disappearance of Russell Hadleigh
2. The Graves of Calgary Bay
3. The Fairy Pools Gathering

Austerley & Kirkgordon Series (Fantasy)

1. Crescendo!
2. The Darkness at Dillingham
3. Dagon's Revenge
4. Ship of Doom

Supernatural and Elder Threat Assessment Agency (SETAA) Series (Fantasy)

1. Scarlett O'Meara: Beastmaster

Island Adventures Series (Cosy Fantasy Adventure)

1. Surface Tensions

Dark Wen Series (Horror Fantasy)

1. The Blasphemous Welcome
2. The Demon's Chalice

Chapter 01

Just how on earth did he end up here? They didn't do frozen food processing that far up in the Highlands, surely. But he was wrong, and the job had come at an opportune moment for Derek. Derek Chef was in fact, ironically, a shift manager in a frozen food processing factory in the Highlands, located just outside of Perth. Derek had come to the plant from Lincolnshire when his previous job had gone belly up.

He'd seen it coming at the old factory. For years, things had been on the slide. They hadn't processed as many vegetables as in previous years. There were also several people in higher positions suddenly leaving. There was no funding for new equipment. No pay rises, even meagre ones.

When the shift managers had gone through the processing season, they'd found that parts weren't as readily available. They were making do—making do eventually just didn't do, and the company started to lose money hand over fist.

There was nothing glamorous in what Derek did. He marched around, making sure people were doing their jobs. The vegetables started at one end and were steam blanched before being put through the large ten-tonne-an-hour freezers. Well, ten tonnes an hour of peas, anyway.

They'd always impressed him, always amazing. Seeing the sheer quantity of vegetables going down a belt into a freezer. Of course, inside the spring-loaded vibration kept them on the move as they were subjected to temperatures into the minus thirties.

And they processed vegetables of all types, from the brassicas at the start of April, to the peas in the main season. Of course, the carrots, parsnips, Brussels sprouts all passing through in the later parts of the year.

Derek enjoyed being a shift manager. It was the banter every day, the back and forth with everyone. Unfortunately, it wasn't always like that, and today Derek was sitting typing up conduct reports.

One thing you had to be as a shift manager was tough on people. If they weren't in the right place, if they were messing about, you had to speak to them fairly and honestly. But you had to wield the axe sometimes, so to speak. He'd fired a few people in his time, and nowadays you had to do it with the shadow of HR on your shoulder. Make sure all the forms had been done correctly, and you had spoken in the correct form and fashion. When Derek had started out in the business, you could have told them to get on their bike. There were no forms back then. It was just a goodbye and I hope I don't see you down the job centre.

Derek looked at the notes in front of him. In truth, it had been one of the more hilarious situations he'd had. Two persons within the company had decided that they rather liked each other. Instead of waiting until they got off shift, they'd decided that they might have a quick moment—hide away somewhere where no one could find them.

Derek had been on his routine checks, and had walked into

the bottom of one of the large freezer units. He didn't enjoy doing it and had to put on a large coat, wrapped up tight, with his helmet on his head, and with a torch. The purpose of the visit was to have a quick scan around to see nothing was wrong, and then get back out quickly before he froze. He got a bit of a shock when he shone his torch into one corner and saw two of his workers wrapped up in each other's arms.

Derek could think of better places for a quick cuddle. Admittedly, it was unlikely that anyone would have found them in there. He didn't want to stay in there longer than he had to and probably after about ten minutes, he wasn't sure if he could move his arms, let alone wrap them around anyone. He laughed to himself when he went home that night, had taken the picture off the wall of his wife and laughed along with her.

Moving up here had been tough; he'd lost a job down there and he'd lost Sandra, but he was still on the go, still making money, and able to live. Many people had it worse. An awful lot of people. Derek sat down by his desk again and then received a knock on his door.

'Come in,' he said.

The man who walked in seemed to Derek to be in the wrong profession. He was a refrigeration engineer, employed by a company to help run the refrigeration plant on site. And he had a rather worried look on his face. Derek had to look up to see this face because Ishmael was six foot four. He was also broad as he came and spoke with a thick, West-Indian accent.

'What's up, Ish?' asked Derek.

'I need you to come and have a look, Derek. Quickly.'

Derek strode back with Ishmael to the refrigeration plant room. Inside, there were many compressors and Ishmael raced

Derek through a variety of dials, pointing out a couple that he wasn't happy with.

'That one there,' said Ishmael.

'The one closest to my office, the one at the back wall.'

'Yes,' said Ishmael. 'I don't know what's wrong with it. This pressure is building in the vessel.'

'Can't you stop it?'

'I'd have to kill the whole plant. I'm trying to switch it off, but it's not the compressor itself. Something's . . . something's building the pressure within it. Something's not feeding correctly. I don't understand, Derek. The computer doesn't agree with the dials.'

'So, what are you telling me, Derek? Are we in a serious situation?'

'We're in a situation. It's all protected, of course. There are relief valves for this. If it over pressurises, it'll blow. You will not get a tank rupture.'

'But if it blows.'

'We'll get ammonia in here. We'll have to evacuate. But we're not there yet. We're definitely not there yet.'

'Well, you can shut the plant before that happens.'

'Like I said, it's not a problem with the plant, Derek. Well, it is. It's just that . . . it's not like I can switch off that compressor and everything's going to stop. The pressure's building. The compressor isn't technically on at the moment.'

'And something's pumping into the—to what?'

'There's a tank behind it. The tank'll blow. Well, the relief valve will blow. We'll get ammonia in here, but there will be plenty of time to clear the factory, I would say. But it will not come to that. I'm going to find it.'

'How long have you got?'

'I should have another half hour.'

'You better get on it, then. I'll go into the office and brief everyone.'

'I'll get on to the boss as well,' said Ishmael. 'See if he's got any ideas.'

Derek walked out of the control room and started marching back to his office. It was a bit of a circuitous route, but it took him back beside the tank, which had the pressure rapidly building inside. It occurred to Derek that he didn't want to be in his office in half an hour's time, but he should be in a distant part of the plant, ready to get everyone out.

Going into his office, he sat down at the desk, picked up his phone, and called the process manager. The young lad, John, had only been with him a couple of years. In fairness, he knew his stuff. He probably knew the refrigeration plant better than Derek did.

'John,' said Derek, as the call went through. 'You need to get down to the plant. Ishmael's got an issue. I don't know what it is, but the big tank, the one beside my office, is starting to over pressurise. He says it won't be unsafe. He says that the relief valve will blow if worse came to worst, and we'd have to evacuate the plant. But, he doesn't know what is causing it. Ish reckons half an hour. He says something's feeding pressure into it.'

'Can't they just cut it off?' asked John.

'I'm not sure he wants to. Maybe he wants to keep the process going. You know what it's like if we have to shut down. Especially if you have to shut down properly. You've got product in the freezer, product on the line. It's not going to last.'

'I'm on my way,' said John.

'I'll meet you in the control room in about five minutes,' said Derek. 'I want to brief everybody else, make sure all the chargehands know that we might have to go to an evacuation.'

'Don't spook everyone, Derek. Tell them not to tell anyone either. Keep everyone going about their business until we get a real handle on this. We want to evacuate at least fifteen minutes before we think it's going to get that bad. And do it in an orderly fashion, Derek.'

'I'm on it, John. See you in the control room.'

Derek put the phone down, picked it up again, and called through to another part of the plant where the vegetables were handled at intake. This call was picked up by Craig, his chargehand.

'Craig, I'll be brief. We've got a problem in the control plant. We may have to evacuate the entire plant shortly. I'll give you the go in about ten to fifteen minutes. Be prepared to get everyone out.'

'What's happening?'

'We may end up with an ammonia leak. Proper one to the point where we may end up just shutting everything down. Don't know at the moment, so don't panic everyone. In fact, don't tell them. Just get yourself prepared to get everyone on the move. Nothing new into the line unless you have to.'

'Understood, Derek.'

Derek sat back in his chair. He'd have to call next door where the freezers were and advise them. He'd get up, walk in and do it. No point in doing it in the office sat beside an ever-increasing risk next door.

He stood up, grabbed his helmet and ear defenders that he had put down after coming back from the control plant. It looked like today could be an interesting one. He walked to the door and then turned and came back, reached inside his drawer, and pulled out a small notebook. It's always good at times like these to have some detail, write down times as things happened. Because if it all stopped, there'd be an enquiry. If there was a leak, you'd have the HSE in, or whoever, wanting to know when things happened. He made a quick note of what he'd just done, of the time he'd spent with Ishmael, and now back here.

The note-taking delayed him by two minutes. As he turned to walk out of the office, it would be the last thing that Derek remembered. The office wall caved in, a piece of it hitting Derek in the head. If he had managed to put his hat on, or his ear defenders, he might have lived to tell the tale.

* * *

Susan Cunningham pulled up on the edge of the factory. The previous day, the place had been in turmoil. Now, there was only a small police presence. There were plenty of others about, the Health and Safety Executive for one. People who knew what they were about. One of them had called the office that day asking for someone to come in because of an issue in this case. Hope had sent Susan, sensing she needed to get out of the office and sending her off to something that wouldn't involve her running around like a lunatic.

Susan was on crutches because of an incident during a previous police case where her leg had been crushed. It was now removed below the knee, and she was waiting to see what they would do. Hopefully, she would get a prosthetic soon so she could get back to looking like a semi-normal person. She'd taken to her crutches well, though, and had grown strong on them.

She'd been reasonably fit to begin with. Her team had been very sympathetic, but she just wanted to get on with it. And Perry, her fellow constable on the team, had been incredibly kind to her. Whenever she needed a lift anywhere, he'd run her there. Even if it was just for groceries outside of work.

Susan got out of her car, thanking the constable for dropping her off. Uniform had been good, too and Macleod had said to use them. DCI Seoras Macleod was the top dog on the murder team, but he had a very hands-off role these days. What he did control was the budget and having a driver for Susan when she required it had been something he'd insisted on.

Susan scooted along on her crutches until she came up to the police cordon.

'Constable Alice Blair,' said a young officer.

'DC Susan Cunningham.'

'I know,' said the woman. 'I heard about your leg. Well, everybody's heard about it.'

'Indeed,' said Susan. 'What can you tell me about here?'

'HSE inspectors are on site. Do you want me to get one of them? They were the ones who were asking for you this morning.'

'If you would,' said Susan. She waited while Alice put a call through. But as Alice finished the call and looked back towards her, Susan could see the pity in her eyes. Susan didn't want pity. She didn't do pity. Susan just wanted to get on.

A man from the HSE arrived shortly. He was around about six feet tall, a thin man, with glasses. He seemed to smile a lot.

'My name's Mark Harrison,' he said.

'Hello, Mark,' said Susan. 'DC Susan Cunningham. You asked for one of our team to come out. You got a problem?

What's going on?'

'Yes,' said Mark. 'Come with me.' He led her to a small hut at the factory entrance and gave her a hard hat. He then walked with her round the side of what was a large vegetable-processing factory.

At the front end, Susan could see tippers used to deposit the vegetables into the line. The vegetables from yesterday were still sitting there. Then came what Mark described as cleaning equipment. Vast, metal objects that Susan was struggling to understand. He then pointed out a section of factory that he said was used to do a basic clean, before the vegetables were put through to the rear section of the factory. That's where the freezers were. When they got round to the side of the first part of the factory, Susan saw a side of the second building blown out by her reckoning.

'It wasn't a massive explosion,' said Mark. 'What you're looking at is the front factory where they clean the vegetables, then the rear factory where they freeze them. Along with the freezing process comes a refrigeration plant. It's a fairly big one this and has vessels containing ammonia. Normally it's all very safe, but one failed during the process. Ruptured.'

'I take it that's not meant to happen.'

'Not at all. The tank shouldn't be a problem. It's over designed for the normal pressure it's meant to hold. You then have relief valves in place. If the pressure gets too high, they blow, not the tank. That will send ammonia gas up into the atmosphere but, as long as it gets up and clear, it blows away; it's designed to do that. Yes, you get a problem, in the sense that you have to tell people to shut their windows, don't go out in it, and it will make people cry. It won't be that bad because it's dispersed up into the air.'

'But you just said that the tank ruptured.'

'Yes, which is a little different because you then get the ammonia within rooms and it can gather and takes much longer to disperse. Which is why it's taken us a while to get in here. However, it's okay at the moment. There are minor residual effects. You may find your eyes beginning to water.'

'Okay,' said Susan, 'but I'm not understanding. You're saying there's been a rupture. Were there any fatalities?'

'One,' said Mark. 'The shift manager, a man called Derek Chef, was in his office. The tank is close to that office. It blew some of the partition through. It looks like he was incredibly unfortunate because part of the wall went into his head, killing him instantly.'

'That is unfortunate,' said Susan. 'A great pity, but at the moment, I'm struggling to understand why I'm here.'

'Well, we looked into the plant systems and what was going on with the refrigeration system. We're still very early days, but it would appear that the over-pressurisation wasn't an accident.'

'What do you mean?'

'The computer system that runs the plant—we think it's been hacked. We think the over-pressurisation of the plant was deliberate.'

'Which means that there may have been an intention to kill,' said Susan.

'There's certainly an intention to cause the over-pressurisation. You tell me what that means. If it's murder, manslaughter, or whatever you guys frame it as. But there's something amiss. There's foul play and because somebody's dead, we called you.'

'I'm going to need to get the team out,' said Susan. 'How much have you contaminated the scene?'

'We've been going about our business and we try to work like your forensics when we realise something is wrong. I've called a halt to a lot of what we're doing. But you'll probably need to work with us on this one,' said Mark.

'Oh, undoubtedly,' said Susan. 'Undoubtedly.'

She scooted closer, taken by Mark into the control room. Susan could feel her eyes beginning to water. He was right about the ammonia. The smell like raw eggs, or rather off-eggs. Mark seemed unaffected.

'Don't worry; you get used to it. That's the tank over there,' he said, pointing at it. A large cylindrical vessel was ruptured on one side. The wall behind it was blown through in parts.

Susan was led by Mark around and through to where she could see into the former shift manager's office. The desk was pushed to one side and there was a mark on the side wall. She could see a light splattering of blood.

As she turned to go, her crutches slipped, and she went down into an expanded V shape with them.

'Can I help you?' asked Mark, reaching for her.

'I'm good. Thanks. I'm good.' Slowly, she pushed herself back up. 'It's just temporary until I get the prosthetic.'

Susan placed a phone call to DI Hope McGrath, her direct boss. She answered quickly.

'What's happening? Will you be back for lunch?'

'Hope, you'll be joining me here for lunch,' said Susan. 'I've got a potential murder.'

'Really?' said Hope.

'You'd better get Ross out, too. I think the computer that ran the factory systems has been hacked. Caused an explosion and one person's dead because of it. Don't know if it was deliberate to kill, or he's a consequence of the action.'

'On our way,' said Hope. 'Get things moving, though.'

'Will do, boss,' said Susan and closed the call down and turned round to see Mark standing there.

'Right, then,' said Susan, 'better introduce me to your team. Mine will be along shortly. I reckon we're going to get to know each other very well over the next day or two.'

Susan smiled. She hated to say it, but as much as one person was dead, at least she felt she was out doing a proper job and hadn't just been sent out of the way until her leg was sorted.

Chapter 02

DS Alan Ross sat in front of the computer, his mind not really focusing on what he was seeing on the screen. Beside him, the computer expert from the HSE, Jamie McIntyre, was explaining what had gone on within the computer system of the refrigeration plant. Jamie was younger than Ross by many years and his computer skills far outweighed what Ross did. That being said, it wasn't as if Ross couldn't follow him. He understood perfectly what Jamie was doing and so far, he had pulled out that the system had been changed by a user named 'JSolace.'

Ross had called Susan Cunningham on the mobile to advise her she needed to find whoever JSolace was. Susan had been with the factory staff, along with Hope and Perry, doing basic interviews, so she should be able to track down the user. Ross had been stuck into the plant's software with Jamie McIntyre and so far it was giving results. Ross, however, had something else on his mind.

He had left his boy at home that morning. He wanted time off because the lad was going to go to the doctor. Hope had insisted that Ross come in because he was the one with the computer expertise on the team. It was the start of the investigation and, first and foremost, they needed to confirm that something had been tampered with. If systems had been running normally, it would just have been an accident.

Ross had come in and asked his partner Angus to reschedule their child's appointment. Not that drastic—it wasn't a life and death situation, but there were indications that Ross's child had abnormal tendencies. Indications showing he wasn't a normal child.

Normal. What did that mean? thought Ross. *Why do we describe it as normal? Just, he was a different child. He would be on the spectrum, they would say.*

Of course, he was way too young to definitely confirm it. But if they could understand him quicker, all the better. There had been difficulties, and Ross had been struggling because he hadn't had time to be at home. He'd gone on these cases, and the case was everything. It was all right for Hope. It was all right for Macleod, Cunningham too, even Perry. None of them had kids.

He was the only one with a kid.

Ross felt the phone go in his pocket, took it out, and realised he'd missed a call. He rang back, and it was Angus on the answer machine.

'Can't get the appointment switched at the moment. We're going to have to go with it, Alan,' said the voice. 'Be there if you can. I understand if you can't. But whatever happens, it'll have to go ahead this afternoon. Well, actually, I'm going out the door now. I'll let you know how it goes if you can't make it. Love you.'

Ross wanted to fling the phone across the room. Wanted to bounce it off the wall but it might have freaked Jamie out sitting beside him.

'That's definitely the hack-in. I think I got the address where it's coming from. It may have been remote to here, but they've used whoever this JSolace is to get in. It's their credentials and their details.'

'I'll take an hour off to try to find them. See if you can see where the link's come from on the outside,' said Ross.

'Well, I'll try. Might take me a bit of time.'

'Well, I'll have to talk to the boss about it,' said Ross. 'I'll touch base with you soon. Things will speed up—always slow at the start of a case.'

Ross fiddled with his tie and his phone in his usual routine and left the small office they were working in.

They stepped out into what was a vegetable-processing factory that wasn't processing. Everything was quiet. There were vegetables sitting, going off in the air. And the smell over the factory was strange to Ross. The sewage treatment plant on site had also been shut down, but it gave a distinct tinge to the air, like things were not wholly abandoned—but the decay had begun; the start of food going off.

Ross walked over to the main suite of the factory offices where Hope had taken up residence. She had taken over their main boardroom, the HSE in a room beside. As he approached, he rapped on the door of the main office and stepped in. In here was a flurry of activity, and he saw Hope at the rear. He waved over to her, and she waved him on in.

'What have you got for me, Alan?' she asked.

'I told Cunningham, it's a JSolace. That's the connection. Their login credentials have been used. I don't know them, though.'

'Good. Have you confirmed if they used any of the business's equipment.'

'It came from off-site,' said Ross, 'still trying to track down exactly where it came from, but you know with these things, you may or may not find it. It may be disguised.'

'Well, I'm not sure if it's murder, or it's culpable homicide, or exactly what we're charging with, said Hope. 'I don't believe it was deliberate. Quite hard to time someone being in, but they may have been doing it with an intention to harm. Reckless for sure. Also, I don't know yet why. We'll pull this Solace person in and see if we can find out.'

Ross went to turn away but Hope stopped him. 'Did you get your appointment changed?'

'No. Angus is off to it now.'

'Are you able to go?' asked Hope.

'I'm needed back there. It's the first day of an investigation. I mean, it's okay.'

'It's not really, is it?' said Hope. 'If you need to go for an hour or two, you can go.'

'It might be longer than that. A couple of hours. Assessments and things and filling forms out. Can't really afford to be away that long.'

'Macleod would let you go. I can let you go.'

'You can't,' said Ross. He turned, shoulders slumped and moped away, heading back towards Jamie McIntyre.

Meanwhile, in another part of the factory, Susan Cunningham was sitting down with the factory boss, Douglas Bradshaw. His official title was the Production Manager, but his role encompassed everything that ran in the factory, including the refrigeration plant and, indeed, the sewage plant.

'He says it's a JSolace, the login that was used to gain access,' said Douglas.

'You know this person?'

'Jane Solace is one of the other factory managers. She works in rotation along with Derek Chef, who died.'

'Is she on site at the moment?'

'No,' said Douglas, 'but she rang today asking if she needed to be in. I said we'd be in contact because you wanted to talk to everyone.'

'Phone her and ask her to come in. We'll need to interview her.'

'Okay,' said Douglas, 'but it won't be Jane. I know it's her login, but why? She would have no reason to.'

'Is Jane liked here? Is she happy?' asked Susan.

'Jane is very well liked here. Jane came through as a bright trainee, a graduate. She's been doing the shift manager role for about a year. It's basically training before she starts to look to move up within the company, head up to sort of my level in maybe the next six, seven years. She's a very good-looking girl, too. Bright, friendly. Everyone likes her. There's not a lot you wouldn't like about her. She's not one of these know-it-alls, either. She's got a way with the factory workers. Can talk on their level. Doesn't talk to them like they know nothing. She realises they know a lot. She gets alongside them; gets on with them.'

'She live local?'

'From away but stays local. No boyfriend or partner that I'm aware of. I've seen her out in the town often too. Seems to have settled into the community. Not like some graduates we get. They come in, breeze through on their way out, think they know everything. And she's done well for herself.'

'Been any romances or anything?'

'No, I mean, she's a good-looking woman. Very good looking, but she hasn't sought to exploit that. She hasn't run around with people. She likes to club, I know that. So she dresses. And she dresses in a fashion that probably is much younger than what I would wear,' said Douglas, laughing slightly. 'But she's not somewhere out on the pull. They still say that, don't they? She's not jumping around from bed to bed or anything. I don't think there's anything in that regard that you would need to know about.'

'And how did she get on with Derek?'

'Well, Derek came up here recently, too. So the two of them started around the same time. Derek had lost his wife, and his job down south. We were fortunate to pick him up. Good shift manager and Jane and him got on well. Never heard a cross word between them. Jane picked his brains. And Derek picked hers, too. Yeah, it was a good match. All my shift managers are.'

'How many have you got?'

'Three. The other one, Ian, is in today.'

'Okay,' said Susan. 'I'm going to get something to eat for lunch. See if we can get Jane in by an hour or so. I'll talk to her then. She'll probably be in with my boss.'

Susan Cunningham disappeared off-site for half an hour to pick up some sandwiches and brought some back for the team. She took one to Hope, passing Perry on the way. DC Warren Perry had been incredibly kind to Susan, of late, and he was turning into an excellent friend. Susan, however, worried that Perry saw her as more than a friend, or at least wanted to. He was a nice enough person, but not the type she would ever go for, with his slovenly ways. She usually liked someone who was neater about themselves, who took a bit more pride in their appearance, but he was being a good friend.

'That's your honey and mustard chicken,' she said, throwing

a sandwich at Perry.

'Thank you. Do you need me to carry any of those around?'

'Got my backpack,' she said to Perry. 'I'm doing the deliveries. Get back on whatever you're doing.'

'More interviews,' he said. 'I hear you got one with the boss.'

'Ross has got a connection,' she said quietly, 'for a JSolace. It's Jane Solace, one of the shift managers. She's coming in. We're going to interview her. You find anything else out.'

'No,' said Perry. 'Staff saw the shift manager walking about. Derek Chef seems to have gone about his normal business. Unfortunate casualty. Not sure he would have been guaranteed to be there. From what they're talking about with the systems, it's unlikely that they could have timed it for Derek to be there. However, it did seem the intention to blow that tank.'

'To do what, then?'

'Highlight stuff? Whatever,' said Perry. 'Ammonia would have gone up, caused a major incident in the town. Everybody would have known about it. Police would have had to go out and shift people massively, tell people to close their windows. Nobody would have died, probably.'

'Ross is touchy again today,' said Susan.

'And he's not happy. He's complaining. Hassling me about it. Oh, for a fag right now.'

'I thought you were off them.'

'I am,' said Perry. He held his hand out. Susan saw it shake slightly. 'Managing,' he said. 'Managing, but yeah.'

'Told you to go on those patches. They would help you.'

'Cold turkey,' he said. 'Two months now. Shakes will go. Trust me, the shakes will go,' he said.

'If you say so.' It was twenty minutes later, when Susan

had done her deliveries and Hope had thrown a vegetarian sandwich down her throat. Together they met Jane Solace, a young woman of only twenty-three years of age. She had long black hair and a face that would have drawn the attention of anyone. Pretty as she was today, her eyes were red.

'And he's dead. Dead because of that.'

'Dead because of the accident, except it's no accident,' said Hope. 'You have a login to the systems, don't you?'

'Yes,' said Jane. She was wearing jeans and a t-shirt with a jumper around her neck. Her face was tired, her hair looking distressed.

'We all have a login. I do. Ishmael does. Derek does. Ian does. Chargehands do as well. The main boss, Douglas, has two. We all got one. We can go into the system. Mine allows me to go into the refrigeration system although I can't, or rather I don't touch anything in there. It's an override to shut it all down that I have. I don't have ways and means to break into the system.'

'Sorry,' said Hope, 'I just want to understand this. You're telling me you don't have a way in which to alter the refrigeration system?'

'No. Why would I? I don't know anything about it. I've learnt a bit,' said Jane. 'Ishmael's taken us round. Took Derek round too. Do I understand fully how the compressors work? No. Do I understand the idea of different loads with different amounts of product coming through? Yes. I understand when we put it under pressure and when it will not cope and how we have to adjust the load going in.

'I understand how the qualities and the amounts of product will work in the refrigeration units. I understand how the refrigeration units work and when they're starting to freeze up—when we're going to have to defrost them, when we're going to have to keep them going, or not keep them going, the pros and cons. But I don't understand how the whole system works. I couldn't make adjustments to it.'

'Someone did in your name,' said Hope.

'But the login system wouldn't allow me to.'

'You have a password.'

'I do,' she said.

'What is that password?' asked Hope.

'I'll write it down,' said Jane. 'It's not easy to remember.' She passed over a piece of paper to Hope, who saw on it different letters, numbers, capitals, exclamation marks, and other symbols.

'You seriously remember that? You type that in every time.'

'Yes. We're not meant to let it out to anyone. I learnt it. You can learn a pattern like that.'

'Anybody else know it?'

'No,' said Jane. 'Nobody knows it. Just me.'

'We're going to have to look at your computer equipment at home. Your phone, your laptop. We're going to have to go through it all.'

'But I have used none of it for any of the systems in here. I don't know how to connect to the system in here. I've no need to,' said Jane. 'I run nothing from home.'

'Nonetheless, it has the ability to do that. And the login that altered the details on the refrigeration plant came from outside of the factory. We're going to need to check all of your equipment.'

Jane leant forward, beginning to cry.

'Do you have anyone close here?' asked Susan.

'What do you mean?'

'Friend? Boyfriend? Partner? Family? Anyone close?'

'What's that got to do with it?' said Jane.

'Nothing,' said Susan. 'Except you could do with someone beside you at the moment. You're in the middle of a bad situation. Our evidence at the moment doesn't say whether or not you put yourself in that situation. But you could do with someone who will bat for you and who will be beside you. You're going to need support over this next while.'

'Nobody,' said Jane. 'I haven't.'

'You'll wait for a moment,' said Susan, 'and we'll get one of our sergeants, DS Alan Ross to come. He'll take you back to your house; he'll pack up your equipment, phones, etc. You'll need to tell other people that you're changing your phone number over. Alan will help you with that, okay? You'll need to pick up a temporary mobile, things like this. Tell the factory here.'

'But all my links are on that, to everyone. It's—'

'Alan will help you. We're not unreasonable, but we need to take away this equipment and check it. If you do anything else between now and the time we do that, Alan has to be there to certify exactly what you've done, and it's for the best purposes of getting you on to other devices to keep your communications going.'

Jane began to cry. 'It's a mess,' she said.

'It is. And in the meantime, don't talk to anyone on site,' said Hope. 'If you need to advise them of coming in or not, everything goes through Douglas at the moment, the factory manager. Douglas will record all conversations between you and him.'

'You know I didn't do this, don't you?' she said. 'Derek was a friend. Derek and I started together here. Derek was good.

And I can't do this. I don't know how to do this.'

'We're investigating Derek's death at the moment. There seems to have been malplay with the factory and with the refrigeration plant that caused Derek's death. We have to get to the bottom of it. If you had nothing to do with it, hang on with us. We'll find that out. Be open and honest. Tell us all you know,' said Hope.

'Detective Sergeant Ross will be here very shortly,' said Cunningham. And with Hope, she left the room, leaving one of the uniformed constables to sit with Jane Solace.

'Well, this just got interesting,' said Hope.

'It did indeed.'

Alan Ross walked into the corridor. 'That was quick,' said Ross.

'I don't think she's our person,' said Hope. 'But, you need to go with her. Get all her equipment from home. We're going to have to go through all of that. Help her change over to a new mobile phone. Whatever. Usual protocols,' said Hope.

'Of course,' said Ross.

'Any word from the appointment?'

'Appointment?' queried Cunningham.

'Oh, the boy's in for an appointment. Sorry, I shouldn't have said that out in front of Susan.'

'It's fine,' said Ross. 'Not yet. Wish I could have been there, though, but . . .' He entered the room that Jane Solace was in.

'It's not getting better with him, is it?' said Cunningham.

'He's missing some family time,' said Hope. 'And I don't blame him on this one. I really don't blame him.'

Chapter 03

Hope McGrath swallowed down the last of her coffee, and stood behind her temporary desk at the factory. She wondered if she could get home that night, and whether John would be there for her. Or would he have fallen asleep when she crawled in during the early hours of the morning? She counted herself blessed, because he usually waited up.

He never complained about what she had to do about her hours of work. Instead, he was just there for her. Ross didn't seem to have the same type of family life and yet she thought Angus was good for him and certainly didn't seem to complain in public. She was trying to understand Ross, and was trying as best she could, but not having a kid, well, that didn't help.

John and she were trying, though. She smiled to herself; this case would not help that. *It changed things,* she thought, *changed from those sudden and magic moments when you started to try to plan. Some of the romance went, possibly. I'll just have to bring it back in.*

She looked up and saw Susan Cunningham entering the office.

'Hope,' she said, 'we're getting reports coming through.

There's been another explosion.'

'What do you mean, *another* explosion?'

'There's a local pharmacy in Inverness. There's been an explosion at it.'

'How do you get an explosion at a pharmacy?' asked Hope.

'I don't know. But I thought you might want to know.'

'Where's Ross?' she asked.

'Still working away with Jamie McIntyre, looking at the software.'

'He's back then from dropping off Jane Solace?'

'I believe they're getting ripped into her computers, or at least getting people who can.'

'I need to see him then.' Hope took off from behind her desk. And as she did so, Susan cleared out of the way in front of her, whirling around on her sticks.

'You're getting a dab hand at those, aren't you?'

'I suppose so,' said Susan. She swished her way out, even holding the door open for Hope as she reached it.

'I suppose so,'—that was her comment, thought Hope. *She was proud of herself before. Delighted. Maybe she's just getting frustrated waiting for the prosthetic. I'll have to monitor that.*

Hope was understanding how Macleod used to feel, keeping an eye on how everyone was at the same time as trying to solve the problem. It was good for you, though; it pulled you back from being entrenched in it. Hope walked around the office block of the factory until she found Ross sitting in a room with Jamie McIntyre.

'How's it going, gentlemen?'

'It's not good,' said Jamie. 'Trying to find where this has come from, it's just, it's not good.'

'Okay,' said Hope. 'Ross, get into Jane Solace's background, through the computer links and that. See if she's been up to anything, if there're any traces to what happened here.'

'Will do,' said Ross. But he was looking away as he said it, and nodded at the computer screen.

'You heard back from our friend?' asked Hope.

'You can call him Angus. It's all right. I don't mind talking about it in front of Jamie. Or telling him about it, anyway.'

Well, that's different, thought Hope. *He's usually such a private guy.*

'Any news?'

'Done their tests. Now they're waiting to give their verdict. They're coming together for that later on today. But I don't know if I'll get there.'

'Well, make the time,' said Hope.

Ross turned, his shoulders slumped, dejected looking. 'I'll try, but I've got Jane Solace to look into now, all the rest of her stuff.'

'And you've got two constables to keep an eye on as well, because I'm leaving.'

'What do you mean, you're leaving?' blurted Ross.

'I need to check on another incident. Susan says there's been a small explosion at a pharmacy near Inverness.'

'Explosion at a pharmacy?'

'Yes,' said Hope. 'That's what I thought. I haven't got a lot more I can do here. You lot are on the case. Better I go check that out rather than take you away from what you're doing.'

'I could do it,' said Ross. 'Be back up towards Inverness. I might pop across—'

'I can't send you up. You need to work with Jamie. You're the one who understands this stuff, not me. I'm the spare appendage at the moment. If it wasn't, I'd be getting Macleod to go and look at it. So no, I'm sorry, but no! That's not going to work.'

'Okay,' said Ross. 'If that's the way it is, that's the way it is.'

Hope left the room, almost kicking herself. *It'll give me a chance to pop in and see Macleod,* she thought. *I'll go to the pharmacy, see Macleod, get back home, then I'll get back down here.*

She had a sudden thought. *Would John be free? Would that work for them? She wasn't sure. Maybe. Maybe there'd be a moment.*

She thought about Ross. *How could she do that? Pop up and then go off and suit her own plans, her own ideas for a family when she was denying him his. Although she wasn't. He was doing that. He was the one who was being a martyr to it. She'd told him to make time, but he wouldn't do it, anyway.*

Hope got into her car and went on the drive up towards Inverness, stopping off at the village just outside the city. It really was a local pharmacy, a classic chemist shop in the middle of a village. Many had closed down, but this one was still open. Outside of it was a lot of police tape. Hope parked her car well short before walking up and approaching the constable. She pulled out her warrant card, but she was recognised almost immediately.

'Inspector McGrath?' said the officer, aware that the public were around.

'Who's looking after the scene?' asked Hope.

'The sergeant's inside. She said to send you through to her when you arrived.'

'Did you know I was coming?' asked Hope.

'The sergeant said you probably would, and when I informed her, the sergeant said to send you to her.'

'Of course. Any forensics on site yet?'

'Jona Nakamura has just arrived with her team. I don't believe she's staying.'

'Excellent. Two birds with one stone,' said Hope.

Hope was shown around the back of the pharmacy and saw the wagon from the forensic unit. Jona was standing at the back of it.

'Are you up here as well?' she said.

'Just wondering,' said Hope. 'I have an explosion at a food processing factory. Now I have an explosion at a pharmacy. Close to each other in timing. Makes me worried.'

'Well, I'll do what I can to find a connection,' said Jona, 'but as far as I understand it, the factory's system was tampered with from outside. Looking at this, it's a tiny explosive device. It's not done a lot of damage and nobody's dead.'

'Could they have been dead?'

'Well,' said Jona, 'the device was planted inside the shop. It blew out, blew the window, blew that corner of the shop, messed everything up and about. You'd have had to be standing right beside it or have got hit in an unfortunate way by glass or wood splinter or something. Much in the same way that unfortunate shift manager died.'

'So, you don't think this is about actually trying to murder people?'

'If it was about sending a signal, nobody put a warning in,' said Jona. 'So, I wouldn't turn around and say it's not about killing people. If you're asking me, was it designed well to kill people? Absolutely not. Which says either it's an amateur or somebody didn't want to kill people, so didn't think of actually getting them out.'

Hmm, she thought. Hope wasn't happy with the answer, although she had no doubt that Jona was right in what she was saying.

'How's Susan getting on anyway with the leg?'

'She's doing well,' said Hope.

'Perry still looking after her?'

'Oh yes, Perry's looking after her,' said Hope. Jona grinned. 'What?' said Hope.

'He's very fond of her, isn't he?' said Jona. 'Not that there's anything wrong with that. But he is—it's just—he has got about twenty years on her.'

'They're just friends,' said Hope.

'Have you seen him lately? Every time he's desperate for a cigarette. Have you seen where his head goes?'

'What do you mean?' asked Hope.

'Perry needs a cigarette. The first person he looks at is Susan Cunningham. That's why he's giving up smoking.'

'He tell you that?'

'No. He didn't. It's obvious.'

Hope grimaced. It wasn't obvious to her. Why wasn't it obvious to her? These were the things that Macleod kept talking about. Things that Hope didn't come up with. They weren't part of an investigation. They were nuances about people that Macleod would have got. Perry would have got it, except Perry was the subject in this case. And Jona. Jona could be as thick as thieves with Macleod when she wanted to. Hope remembered when the two of them would go off to meditate. Macleod could never meditate with anyone else.

'I've left a couple of my guys in there working away on it. I'm not sure what this is about. Also not sure when it was planted, but we'll have some answers for you soon.'

Hope went to the shop and saw the sergeant there.

'Hello,' said the sergeant. She was short, maybe only five

foot two, and had to look up to six-foot Hope. She had blonde hair, and Hope could see that she was pregnant by maybe four or five months.

'Hope McGrath.'

'Sergeant Ellie Gold.'

'Congratulations. I see you're in the way,' said Hope.

'Thanks. Although I'm not sure how much longer I'm going to be doing this. Anyway, it doesn't seem like anybody was hurt by this one. The cashier was the only one in the shop at the time. She was attending to work in the pharmacy. She works both as it's quiet at this time of day. There are a few assistants, but they're not working at the hour the bomb exploded.'

'Have you taken a statement?'

'Statement from her, getting in touch with customers who were in this morning, running through her staff. We'll get all the details, but to be honest, it looks like I might have pulled you up here for nothing.'

'It's unusual though,' said Hope, 'to get an explosive positioned in a place like this. I mean, why? It makes little sense.'

'No,' agreed the sergeant. 'Nice building though.'

'Yes it is,' said Hope. 'It doesn't look the same as the rest of the street. Well, it does. It looks the same, it's just not, well, the same, is it? It's more, well, newer.'

'Last one burnt down. They had to demolish it, so this was put back in its place. Done a good job of it, though. Well, until they blew the window out this morning.'

'Get the statements and put the report down to DC Warren Perry. Copy everything across to him. If we can also see what security footage you've got. I notice there are CCTV cameras about. If it's still intact, send that down to Susan Cunningham in my team, too.'

'Will do' said Ellie.

'Otherwise,' said Hope, 'I'll get off. Going up to see the head honcho on this one today.'

'Pass my regards to DCI Macleod. Those of us on the ground are happy he came back from the last one.'

Ellie was referring to the last case the team had undertaken where Macleod had been an eventual target. They'd lost one member of the force during that investigation. And Macleod had spoken eloquently at the funeral.

'Well, thanks for that,' said Hope, 'I'll do that.'

Hope departed the village, getting back to Inverness Station and finding Macleod in his office.

'So, what have we got?' asked Macleod.

'I've got two explosions now.'

'I think I heard.'

It wasn't that close to Macleod. Hope grinned. Macleod's efforts at humour were usually pretty poor.

'The one down at the frozen food factory,' said Hope, 'that's definitely malicious. And the one closer to home here looks like it's malicious too, because Jona says it was a bomb. She's still working on the type and that, but definitely an explosion from a device.'

'Close in time together too,' said Macleod.

'We got a suspect we're chasing down,' she said. 'But to be honest, I don't think she did it. Somebody hacked in from the outside into the refrigeration plant. I'm just not convinced. Don't know where, and we don't know who. This latest one, we're only just getting started.

'Need any other help. These things are quite spread out regarding their locations.'

'If I do, I'll ask for it,' said Hope. 'One thing that bothers me is Ross's state of mind is still not good.'

'Is his work suffering?'

'No, but his home life is. He was meant to go to a meeting today about his kid with the hospital or a specialist or something.'

'Looking to see if he's on the spectrum. I heard that.'

'Well, I told Ross to go. He wouldn't do it. And then he's bitter and complaining about the—'

'Ross won't go anywhere unless you tell him and order him with force. You might have to do that. But truth be, at the moment, if you've got people hacking in from the outside, you're going to need Ross with you. He's the one on the team that understands that. I'd fill in, but I think I'd be frankly useless,' said Macleod.

'I don't say that often about you, Seoras, but I agree.'

'Well, let's keep going at the moment. I don't like the idea of a second explosion.'

'I'm not sure the first one was meant to kill,' said Hope. 'I think it was an accident that it did. Reckless, but an accident. The second one didn't hurt anyone but wasn't meant to, given its size.'

'Well, get on it. You don't want it to become a habit. Explosions panic people. A panicked public draws attention from upstairs. Makes the case harder to deal with. You know what happened last time? They got panicked upstairs.'

'I still say I could have handled that case.'

'And so do I,' said Macleod. 'Although you wouldn't have come up with the mannequin's head.'

Macleod had been in a small tunnel, his head apparently put through a gap and then taken off with a large, swishing knife. It was one of many mechanical devices involved in the case. Macleod had switched his own head with the tailor's dummy's head, giving the impression that he'd been decapitated. Clarissa still hadn't forgiven him.

'Don't let me keep you,' said Macleod. 'I'm here if you need me.' Hope thanked him and walked out of the office.

She got to her car and looked at the time. She could get home. Yes, she could. We'd only have an hour. Half an hour? Half an hour would be enough.

She placed a call to John on her mobile. As soon as he answered, her hopes fell flat.

'Somebody's had a crash in one of the cars. I'm dealing with it,' he said. 'I can't get away at the moment.' John ran a hire car firm and was the boss.

'Pity,' said Hope.

'You're telling me,' said John. 'I could do with seeing you at the moment. This crash has got me.'

'Soon,' said Hope. She got into her car and thought about the drive back down to the factory. Ross was right. This job sucked sometimes.

Chapter 04

Hope arrived bright and early the next morning at the factory, entering the offices and finding her makeshift desk. She sat down, awaiting the arrival of the rest of the team. She lodged up in a local hotel and she hadn't caught up with John, but had a long conversation until about two in the morning.

It wasn't the same. She'd got her hopes up and she wanted to be with him. Yet Hope realised that the half hour they would have had would have been a functional thing. That was the thing; you decided to have a kid, and suddenly, you had to make time for each other. You were formally getting together to create something.

She laughed at herself. She was constantly putting words together that weren't natural, weren't right. When you want to make love, it should be on the spur of the moment. It should be that or incredibly well anticipated, after a night together of walking, talking, dining, whatever. That or a passionate explosion.

They had chatted for a long time and talked a lot about Ross. He wasn't giving the best impression for two would-be parents. He was, however, thankfully unaware. She was worried about him, but he was first in that morning, right behind her.

Ross came in, tie and suit as usual and began making the coffee only to realise that Hope had done it.

'How are you today?' she asked him.

'I missed it yesterday,' he said. 'I missed it. Angus isn't happy.'

'I don't blame him. You need to go.'

'I can't. You know that? I can't. This is what I do. This is what I am.'

'What you are?'

'Yes,' said Ross. 'Like Macleod. It's what he is. It's why he hasn't retired.'

'This can't be what you are. It can be what you do. But it can't be what you are,' said Hope. 'You're a dad. That's what you are. You're a dad.'

Within half an hour, Hope had the team all sitting around a large table.

'So let's catch up. Where are we? Ross, you start.'

'Jane Solace,' said Ross. 'We know it was her login that was used to get into the system and then change the parameters.'

'How easy is it to change the parameters?' asked Hope.

'Once you're in, it's very easy to understand,' said Ross. 'With somebody like Jane, she already had a working knowledge of the system.'

'Jane had a working knowledge of the system?' asked Perry. He was sitting, twiddling his thumbs, while he asked Ross this. It was a thing with Perry now. He seemed a little more on edge. Not with his mind and not with his interactions with people—he just seemed on edge. Hope put it down to the lack of nicotine in his system. Hopefully, it would be something he would sort out.

'You could run it. The basic idea of how the system works.

You could cause this,' said Ross.

'Aren't there any safeties to say they shouldn't?' asked Perry.

'Well, that's the thing. They've gone into the actual program. The intention was never for the likes of Jane or Derek or anything. We can't find that on anybody else's except for Douglas Bradshaw, the factory manager. But we find no login from him on that day, or even the month before. He didn't have access to the login details of Jane Solace. Nobody does except the administrator, who is sitting at this point in time in Belgium.'

'And they wouldn't have a good reason to destroy their own work,' said Hope.

'They're trying to sell more of the systems they put in. It's not that old, a couple of years. But this hack doesn't look good for them. It's starting to put people off. It's a repeated system as well.'

'So, what about her own background? Did you find anything out from her PC or phone?'

'A lot,' said Ross. 'She's got a history of minor cyber crimes and she's got frequent visits to anarchist forums.'

'That's funny, because I wouldn't have thought she'd be like that,' said Hope.

'She seemed incredibly pleasant,' said Susan Cunningham. 'I wouldn't have clocked her for that.'

'What sort of thing?' asked Hope.

'Well, the sort of cyber crimes I'm talking about, they're very basic. She's done hacks. Hacks on certain sites. Well, I say hacks, it's not. It's comments, been part of a group to overload a site with comments to take it down. Most of these sites have been quite nationalistic, BNP, stuff like that.'

'You said anarchist forums as well, though,' said Hope

'There's a history there of visiting them, but the sort of sites she's in don't talk about explosions. They talk about general unrest, things like computer systems coming down. Just talk about how to do it but there's nothing in her history and nothing in the way she uses those laptops to say that she has the capacity to do what this person did to the system.'

'Were there any links from the laptop into the computer system in the factory?'

'None. It's not coming from there. It's clean. All her devices are clean on this. Maybe she's got other devices stored away somewhere else, which is always a possibility. The ones she's using at home are not involved.'

'But,' said Perry, 'if she was hiding this ability, wouldn't that be what you would do? You would set it up somewhere else, using a completely different laptop, go in, and then make it look like you were set up.'

'How easy would it be to get the password of somebody else? How easy would it be to go in and fake it?' asked Hope.

'You'd have to break into the system,' said Ross. 'No evidence of that, but somebody really good could do it without leaving evidence. That's the problem.'

'The thing is,' said Hope, 'the actual explosion fits the motive with regards to these anarchist sites. It doesn't look like anybody was intentionally trying to kill someone here. It was an incredible fluke that meant that Derek died. So, in that regard, what actually happened here ties in very well with what she is.'

Susan Cunningham suddenly gave out a large yawn.

'Are you all right? Not boring you, are we?'

'Sorry,' said Susan. Hope looked over at Perry. Jona was right. He was gazing at her.

'Okay?' asked Perry.

'I'm fine,' said Susan. 'Really, I'm fine. Sorry, Hope. Go on.'

'What about our reports from up the road? What have we got from there?' asked Hope.

Jona was sitting at the table. 'The explosion up the road was not set to kill anyone. It was, however, a well laid-out piece of kit. The explosion could have hurt someone, but they'd had to be really close to it.'

'And where did it come from? What was the equipment that did it? Purchased? Anything on that?'

'It's the thing that's getting me,' said Jona. 'It's not that sophisticated. In a lot of ways, it's a very crude bomb. The timer, the actual explosive, not that hard to get hold of. I think it may have been stolen. There are reports of explosives being nicked from a quarry.'

'From a quarry? Those would have done a lot more damage,' said Hope.

'Unless you leave most of it behind and just use a little,' said Jona. 'Somebody understood, I think, the proportion of explosives to the effect. The bomber was somebody quite smart.'

'That fits Jane Solace's profile as well. She is smart.'

'Maybe it's part of a team,' said Ross. 'Maybe she's running with someone.'

'You mean with the anarchists?' said Perry. 'It's a good idea, but I don't agree with it.'

'Have you met the woman?' asked Hope.

'No,' said Perry. 'However, the impression I've got from her colleagues is that she's a good person. Groups are not her at all. She's very independent. She gets on with a lot of them, but when she asks questions and gets alongside, she still has an independent core. There's a part of her you never get to. The type of woman that they're describing wouldn't work well on a team. She'd learn off them, but she wouldn't be part of a team with them. In fact, I'm not sure how she would do here, except that she seems to function as the head, in whatever she does.'

'Well,' said Hope, 'we haven't got enough to tag onto her yet either. All we know is it's her login that was used.'

'I talked to the HSE,' said Jona. 'I can confirm that Derek Chef was not killed maliciously, or at least not with any precision. A flying piece of metal drove its way into his brain. Died instantly. He was well liked, too.'

'Something to think about,' said Perry. 'We've had two explosions. Pharmacy, food process plant. Totally different places. Totally different scales. Totally different locations. Are we jumping to conclusions trying to make a link?'

'I'm not making any conclusions,' said Hope. 'But two explosions like this, close together? Also the second one—that's obviously some sort of cry for attention. And the first one would have been if Derek hadn't had died; the HSE would have come in and said, somebody has hacked into your computer system. The ammonia would have gone up and you would have had the whole of the town knowing about this explosion. It would have been an evacuation.'

'Well, that's what happened anyway, isn't it?' said Ross.

'Yes, but it would have been planned. It would have been planned. This one here. It's strange isn't it? But all you've got to do is set off the pressure relief valve and everybody's running out.'

'But it doesn't look like an accident then' said Perry. 'Or rather, it looks like an accident. It doesn't look like they're making a point. Enormous hole in the side of a tank makes a point.'

'So, basically,' said Hope, 'we're struggling to understand why at the moment.'

'Well, we'll get into it,' said Susan. Hope looked over at her and noticed the dark circles under her eyes. Ross, meanwhile, held his head, looking out the window.

'Back to it, then,' she said. 'See what else we can dig up, okay? But not you, Susan. I need a word with you before you go.'

'I'll get your lunch for you,' Perry said to Susan. 'Maybe take a rest at lunchtime.'

'I'm fine, Perry. All right? That's enough. I'm fine.'

'Just asking,' he said.

The team cleared the room, leaving Susan with Hope.

'How're you getting on?' she asked.

'Swimmingly,' said Susan. 'Look, I'm good to go.'

'Sit down a minute,' said Hope.

'Sit down? Have I done something wrong?'

'No, you haven't. You're doing everything very well. Except for one thing.'

'And what's that?'

'Telling me you're fine. You're not. You never come in with bags under your eyes. You haven't slept last night. I don't know why not, but you haven't—'

'It's fine.'

'It's not fine,' said Hope. 'We're all under pressure at the moment for different things.'

'Work's fine. I didn't have a problem coming down here taking on the case and bringing you all in.'

'Pressure isn't from work,' said Hope. 'Listen, John and I, well, we want to start a family. I was hoping yesterday I might get some time with him. Didn't happen. We were up to two in the morning talking about it. That's not something I share with anyone, so you keep that to yourself. Ross is struggling. Fatherhood is causing him problems. He's not getting away to deal with certain things and really not setting me a great example. Perry's struggling because he's giving up his cigarettes. He's doing that for you,'

'I know,' said Susan. 'At first it was quite cute, but it's not cute anymore. He needs to do it for him.'

'Couldn't agree more,' said Hope. 'Maybe you need to talk to him about that.'

'Maybe,' said Susan, 'but I don't want to,'

'What?' asked Hope.

'I do like him; he's nice. I'm not ready yet, and I'm not saying I ever will be. This leg needs sorted first.'

'When's it happening?'

'Another month or two? That's when they're talking about the prosthetic, getting it sorted, anyway.'

'And how are you coping?'

'Well, I get about, don't I?'

'No. Not about that,' said Hope. 'How are you coping with—?'

'Well, I'm not, am I? At least I was. I'm not anymore.'

Hope sat back. She'd made the breakthrough, but she'd done it in her way. Constant questions, one after another. Keeping going, keeping asking. Macleod, Perry, Jona. They would have sussed what was going on. They'd have been able to broach it quickly. But Hope had to work through her line of attack.

'What's up?'

'I didn't sleep last night,' said Susan. 'I was back there. I was back there with the wall. And the wall fell on my leg.'

Cunningham shook. 'And the pain ripped up through me again. Perry was there, pulling me along. Helping me out. And you were there, too. But afterwards, I couldn't get up. I couldn't walk away. I ended up in a cold sweat.'

'There are people who can help you with this sort of thing. I can refer you,' said Hope.

'What's your weirdest dream?' asked Susan suddenly.

'Don't really get weird ones,' said Hope.

'You know what my weirdest one has been?' said Susan. 'I attended the funeral for my leg last night. We buried it in a coffin. You were all there, standing, saying goodbye to it. But I couldn't. It was last night, Hope. That's my issue. I think you're right. I think I need to see someone.'

'I'll get on it,' said Hope. 'Get you referred.'

Susan stood up from the chair and went with her crutches out through the door. She stopped just before she left the room.

'Keep asking. It helps.'

Hope nodded. At least she was getting something right.

Chapter 05

Hope could hear the banging at her door. She was in a hotel room and she checked her phone, but there was no message. That was strange. If something had happened in the case, the first thing that she would have got was a text or a phone call advising her.

She threw off the bed sheets, wrapped herself up in her dressing gown, and walked across to the bedroom door. Hope had her dressing gown with her, the small one that John liked, which stopped about mid-thigh. She happily walked round the house in it, with only his eyes to see.

Right here, on a case, she'd only wear it in the hotel room. A reminder of him, that's what it was.

She put a bleary eye up to the peep hole. Her heart skipped a beat. She tried to let her eye clear, become less blurred, and John's smiling face appeared there.

She opened the door quickly. He raced in and she shut the door behind him, before he flung his arms around her, pulling her close.

'What are you doing here?' she asked.

'What do you think I'm doing here? We couldn't get the time, but I'm not working tomorrow. I thought I can come here, and we can do what we need to do for as long as we want to do it. I can get back up the road and crash in tomorrow morning. Or I can just sit with you, or we can—'

Hope didn't let him finish. Instead she was kissing his lips, pulling at his t-shirt.

'Shut up,' she said. 'Just shut up.'

'I'm shutting up.' He picked her up, which was never a simple task for him, because she was slightly taller. His hands underneath her thighs, he carried her across the room and tried to elegantly place her on the bed. However, he ended up dropping her, and she laughed as he then threw himself on top of her.

'Missed you,' she said quickly.

'Well, that's evident.'

Her mobile phone vibrated.

'That can sod off,' she said.

John had stopped for a moment.

'I said, it can sod off.'

'You better take it,' he said.

'I decide if I take these things. I said it can sod off. Your job is here with me.'

'Hope,' said John. 'It's half-past one in the morning. They don't call you at half-past one in the morning unless something's happening. It's not a random text.'

Hope rolled over on the bed as John held himself above her. She picked up the mobile phone and looked at it.

'Bollocks,' she said. 'Buggery bollocks.'

'Want me to wait,' he said.

'I don't know. There's been an explosion. It's at a primary school.'

'Hell,' said John. 'Anyone—'

'Done during the night. No one injured.'

'Are they needing you right away?' asked John.

'Seoras wants to meet me.'

'You're kidding,' said John.

'No, Seoras wants to meet me. I'm going to have to drive up to Inverness. Might be heading over to Stornoway tomorrow.'

'Are they all connected?' asked John.

'I don't know,' said Hope. 'There are a lot of explosions happening very close together, timewise. If they're not connected, it's a heck of a coincidence.'

'If you're going up, I'll drive you up. You can sleep on the way up.'

'No, you get some sleep,' she said. 'You've got—'

'I don't have to go into work tomorrow,' said John. 'That's why I came down here. I'll drive you up.'

She sat up on the bed, and pulled him close, hugging his head into her bosom. She kissed the top of his head. 'I'm sorry. I'm sorry,' she said. 'I was so—'

'Yeah, I got that bit,' said John. 'I really did. It'll happen,' he said. 'It'll happen. And then they'll have to look after you. Then you really will have to have time off in a way. And they won't be able to stop you. It'll be a legal right.'

'I need to pack some stuff up and that. I don't know where I'm going to end up tomorrow.'

'Pack away,' said John. 'Anything I can do for you.'

'No,' she said and turned and started taking out some clothing and laying it on the bed. John rolled over, sat at the top end, watching her.

Hope casually removed her clothing and then changed, her eyes focusing on John a lot of the time. He was smiling as he watched her, but the excitement had worn off. He watched her get changed every day. This just felt like another normal day.

'You ever get annoyed with my work?'

'Of course not,' said John. 'This is a part of you.'

'Ross told me it was who he was.'

'No,' said John. 'It's what you do, not who you are.'

'That's what I told him.'

Half an hour later, Hope was sitting in the passenger seat of her car as John drove it to Inverness. As he said, the beauty of being in charge of a hire car firm meant that he could extend his hire car lease so he could leave it down at the hotel.

It was five o'clock in the morning when Hope reached the police station. She sent John to the canteen while she made the trip up the steps to Macleod's office. His secretary wasn't in because she kept normal hours, something he'd insisted on.

But the office door was cracked slightly ajar, and a light could be seen from inside. It was summer, but that side of the building didn't get the morning light and so his office light would be on. She pushed open the door.

'Sorry,' said Macleod.

'It's my job. You don't have to apologise.'

'You arrived in your car and you got out of the passenger side. John got out of the driver's side. I'm sorry.'

'Does nothing get past you,' asked Hope.

'No, of course not.'

'What do we know?'

'What I know is I am getting a stack of pressure. I've been in here for the last two hours, getting it in the neck from politicians, from the high heidyins. I am getting it in the neck from everywhere.'

'What do you want us to do?'

'Well, that's up to you. It's your team; you deploy them. You don't worry about me getting it in the neck. That's why I'm here. I'm your foil. We've talked about this before.

'What I don't understand,' said Macleod, 'is, we're here, there, and everywhere with these explosions. They're now targeting a school. That's going to get people's backs up. Maybe that's the point of it.'

'It's done in the middle of the night; nobody is about. Think about it, Seoras. I don't believe,' said Hope, 'that this person was intending to kill anyone. Even down at the food factory, I believe it was an accident. I think it was elaborate what they were doing with the system. Maybe they couldn't get in properly, and they did it from a distance. There's no link for Jane Solace, as far as we can tell, to the pharmacy. This is somebody else with a different intention. At least that's what it looks like.'

'Well, unless you don't fully understand her intentions yet; don't rule her out.'

'Of course not. But I'm thinking.'

'What?' asked Macleod.

'We're going to be split up here. We've now got people on the loose everywhere. I'm going to end up having to send people over to Stornoway. Keep somebody down at the factory. Keep—'

'This is why I wanted you in. Stop,' said Macleod.

'It's the right thing to do,' she said. 'It's—'

'Stop,' said Macleod. He stood up, and opened the door of his office again. Macleod marched out, then came back in a couple of minutes later.

There was a large cafetiere of coffee, and he poured a cup for Hope and one for himself. He sat down and looked at her.

'Explosions are happening. You're going in as you always do and you're following the line of attack. What can I discover; what's there? Oh look, somebody's broken into a system. We go down the lines of chasing them up. We then look at their hardware, software. Does that provide any links? Get people on the ground. Boots out there.'

'Well, that's my job,' said Hope.

'Stop,' said Macleod. 'What do you think I would do?'

Hope looked at him. 'What do I think you would do? I'm not you. I'm not going to follow you. I'll get on the blower and ask Perry. That's why you gave me Perry, wasn't it? So, he would give me what you gave me. That's what you said.'

'Yes, that's why I gave you Perry. But this isn't about Perry or what I can give you in that sense. This is about you running an investigation. You can't, when you run an investigation, simply follow the procedure down. You've got to look at it. Need to anticipate what's coming up. You need to try to be one ahead because somebody's yanking your chain.'

'The only person who's yanking my chain is you getting me up here in the middle of the night.'

'I'm sorry about that,' said Macleod. 'Really sorry about that. I didn't realise.'

'Realise what?' asked Hope.'

'It's not my place,' said Macleod. 'Nowadays, you're not meant to even mention it.'

'Mention what?' said Hope.

'Let's say I wish you every success. It's something I never managed. So, I wish you success.'

'How do you do that?' asked Hope.

'I read people. And I've been working with you for how long? I see the signs; I see the clues. John does not race down to you when you are away working. Can't think of when he did before. You came up yesterday to see me. You then left and went straight back. But before you did, you were in the car park, and you took a phone call you were upset with.

It was short and you went straight back down the road. And I thought you might have popped in to say hello at least. Now looking at it, I'm putting two and two together; yes, I'm sorry I interrupted you.'

'That's quite scary. I hope you haven't been watching me.'

Macleod laughed. 'I don't need to watch you,' he said. 'But back to my main point. You need to react. So, you need to think about what's coming. What have we had so far?'

'Well, we've had three explosions,' said Hope.

'And what's been the defining factor about all three?'

'I don't know,' said Hope.

'Yes, you do. What do they all have in common? When you get an explosion—one explosion—you're looking for an accident. When you get three, and you know the first one wasn't an accident, what are you looking for?'

'A reason,' said Hope.

'You're telling me you don't think anyone was meant to die. Why cause an explosion then? What's the point?'

'To flag something up, to make a point.'

'Exactly,' said Macleod. 'Nobody's made a point yet. Nobody has turned round and said, "This is why I'm doing this." Or even given us an idea about it. It's coming. It's coming soon. Three explosions. You've got to explain yourself. Even terrorists announce it was them. There's no point causing terror if nobody knows who to be afraid of.'

'So, what are you thinking?' asked Hope.

'I'm thinking that you don't go too far, and you prep yourself.'

'Ross can do most of his stuff online. I'm going to send him over to the school.'

'Why?' asked Macleod.

'One, he's good at all that. And he'll round things up. He can use the Stornoway crew. Alan's worked with them before over there. He's been with you and me longer than anyone.'

'That's true,' said Macleod. 'But what's the real reason?'

'The real reason is that he needs to find purpose in what he's doing again. Everything he's doing has been about his kid. His kid has been influencing him. These are some kids under attack. It might help him.'

'It's good thinking,' said Macleod. 'That's not something I would have come up with. Jane probably would have.'

'Maybe you should bring her in more often,' said Hope.

'What's the rest of your plan?' asked Macleod.

'I've got to find a connection. Got to get Susan and Perry on to that. They can go through all the interviews, see if it's small, see if it's tenuous, see if it's—'

'It won't be tenuous, but it might be obscure,' said Macleod. 'Food factory. Pharmacy. School. All of them are good things and have very different people within them. All of them do a separate function. It will be obscure, or at least difficult to uncover. Otherwise, we'd be shouting at it. The papers won't have a clue what's going on, so they'll just put in wild theories.'

'Anything else you want to talk to me about?'

'What are you off to next?'

'I need to head back down to my hotel, get the team tomorrow, maybe get Ross on the ferry.'

'Get Ross to get a flight over,' said Macleod. 'You can stretch the budget. Use the team there. Maybe pick up someone to go over with him from Jona.'

'Will do,' said Hope. 'If there's not anymore, I'll get back down the road.'

'Can I just say one thing?'

'What?' asked Hope, looking a bit agitated.

'When I was on cases, Jane learnt I wasn't available. Jane and I were never as young as you two. And we weren't looking to start a family.' Macleod stared at Hope as intently as he ever did. 'Don't put this stuff aside. I don't know how you do it, but you need to make time. If it's what you want in your family life, it's what you want. Just make it happen.'

'Thank you, Seoras,' she said, 'thank you for your concern. It's touching.'

'I have plenty of regrets in my life, Hope. I don't want you to have too many.'

'You didn't go into any detail of how to make this time, or how to fit in any of the actions. For that, I am so glad.'

Hope stood up, walked over to the door. As she opened it, she felt something soft hit the back of her head. She turned and looked down at the floor, and saw Macleod had thrown one of his gloves at her.

She smiled at him. 'Seriously though, thank you.'

Macleod nodded. 'Enjoy the drive.'

Chapter 06

It was two days later when it arrived. Ross had been over to Stornoway and indeed, there had been an explosion at the school. The device was like the one found at the pharmacy and it had clearly been timed to cause no human harm. The school was completely closed up and it being the middle of the night, no one was there. It blew out the side of a classroom and some children were deeply disappointed to have had their schoolwork destroyed. However, the school was closed the next day, which meant some kids were quite happy.

Ross, however, was fed up at going over. Hope's plan to have him work amongst the children was not a success when she spoke to him after he came back. He walked in that morning, having arrived late the previous night back on the plane.

'So how are you?'

Ross walked past her. 'I'm here. . . . Bit of a wasted trip. Didn't really need me out there. Wasn't much going on. The forensic team could have handled it.'

'I needed somebody out there. But at least we know the children were safe.'

'I don't get it,' said Ross. 'Why do that? What's it represent?

Says nothing. You just blew up a classroom. You blew up a pharmacy. One teaches; the other gives out medicine to the sick. Closed it for a couple of days, both of them. He shut down a plant that makes frozen vegetables. Why? None of these are evil organisations. None of these are doing anything underhanded. Why would you bother?'

'It's what we need to find out,' said Hope.

'Well, I'm not seeing anything at the moment,' said Ross. 'But I'll get on it. I'll get on it again.'

'It's not just you that needs to be on it but the entire team,' said Hope.

'Yeah, well. Let's see if Perry can analyse a building or its history. He's better with people, so I'm told.'

Hope went to stop him, but she didn't know what to say. They would rely on Ross for this. Tracing the records. If they gave it to Susan or to Perry, they'd have to get someone else to help them with it. It wasn't what they were good at. Hope turned to go back to her office, but then Susan Cunningham walked into the main office. Hope couldn't help but notice the grimace on her face.

'You all right?'

'It's the pain. I don't know where this pain's coming from. I haven't had pain for, well, since it happened. I know there's pain.'

'Where?' asked Hope.

'That's the thing. Down there.'

'Where? You've got a pain in your—'

'I've got a pain in the missing bit of my leg,' said Susan. 'Makes little sense, does it?'

'Well, on the face of it, no. But you have been—'

'I have been through significant trauma. Everywhere I go,

everybody says to me, "Susan, you just have to wait. You've been through significant trauma." Well, I'm sorry. I'm fed up with significant trauma. I need to get on.'

She went to step forward on her crutches, but suddenly seemed to buckle up. Perry came into the room behind her. Quickly, he put two arms underneath her shoulders, supporting her.

'Let's get you down to the table.'

'Thanks, Perry.'

Hope watched as Perry effectively carried Susan down and deposited her in her seat beside her desk. There was a sudden intake of breath by one of the uniformed constables assigned to the team at this time. Hope recognised her as being quite new, and she turned round to find someone standing right beside her at the door into the main office. Hope wondered what had shocked her and then saw the face of Macleod.

'Easy, Perkins,' she said. 'it's only the DCI.'

'I need a word,' he said. Hope could see he had a large envelope inside a plastic packet.

'Of course,' she said. She hurried through into her own office with Macleod following, and he shut the door behind him, effectively letting her know that this was serious.

'It's arrived,' he said.

'What's arrived?' asked Hope.

'I said it would arrive. I said we would get the information, and it's here.' He pulled a brown envelope out from a plastic packet and from inside, he produced two sheets of photocopied paper. On them was the image of a letter in colour.

'It's not as good as the original, but Jona's got the original and is going over it with a fine-tooth comb. The colour is a little darker than what the original is, but you can see the style of the handwriting and can get the words.'

'Okay. What does it say?'

'Read it,' said Macleod.

I did it. I was the one who planted those bombs. I was the one who caused the explosion. I'm sorry for the man who passed away, but it doesn't detract from my point. And more will die when I make my final point in the grand finale. I could just tell you what's wrong, but I fear you'd find me then. And I don't want that. I do, however, want those who caused my pain to suffer. I would tell you as we go along what I intend to do, but I fear you won't listen. I fear your only concern will be for me. It's taken time to plan this, but I'm set and I'm ready. No doubt you now have the case. It's always you on the telly and if it's not, you'll know who has it. War will come. War will be done. Welcome to Boomtown.

Signed, *Your friendly, Explosive Activist.*'

'Wow,' said Hope. 'More to come.'

'Exactly. I've got Jona analysing the letter. She's getting a handwriting expert on it because it is handwritten. She's also going to search the letter for any telltale signs.'

'But in the meantime,' said Hope, 'we need to find them before—'

'Before they plant another device. This is the problem,' said Macleod. 'I keep rereading it. There are not many clues. It's someone who's been wronged. That's clear. They feel aggrieved because nobody's taken up their cause. Is it an aggrievement against them, specifically, or is it, I don't know, because he didn't watch out for the whales on the shore? It's nothing, absolutely nothing. No indication about why he's planted these bombs in these places.'

'It's a strange letter,' said Hope, 'because for one talking about injustice, he's planted it in a school, a pharmacy, and a frozen vegetable plant. I don't see that they've done much to the public except feed them, cure them, and teach them.'

'Well, the school system might not be what it used to be,' said Macleod, 'but I don't think it's killing children.'

'I'll show the team,' said Hope. 'See if they can get a take on it.'

'And how are they?'

'They're here. They're working.'

'Do you want me in with you when you do it?'

'No,' said Hope. 'I don't think so. I don't think I need you in.'

'Okay,' said Macleod. 'I understand. Make sure you use them, though. Make sure you get the best out of them. We're going to need it.'

Macleod turned to walk away and then stopped. 'This will probably mean a few more late nights. I wouldn't normally say this but—'

'I'm well aware of the fact. What will be said in the papers if I was found to be starting a family at the time I was meant to be responding to an explosion,' said Hope. 'I know you hoped to put it delicately, but there's no other way to it. Seoras, I'm a DI; I get that. You remember I handle the media much better than you do.'

'Guilty as charged,' said Macleod. 'Want me to stop watching out for you?'

Hope ignored the comment. 'You were right about the letter, though,' she said. 'So what's he doing next?'

'He blows somewhere up,' said Macleod. 'Not sure it's going to be anything obvious.'

'Why?' asked Hope.

'Everything he's done has been on the quiet. First one, he hacks in through the internet. He doesn't have to be there, though I want to know how he got in.'

'And the next two, what, he just walks in and plants them?'

'Quite possibly. Did we get anywhere with CCTV?'

'No. Nothing. I have picked nobody out that looks suspicious.'

'The school he could pop into at night and set it off, but there was no sign of break-in, was there?' asked Macleod.

'There was a door that was unlocked; he could have gone in. In fact, there were a couple. It's an island school; it's out of the way; it's not really used that much by many people. But come on, it's the Isle of Lewis. You know what it's like.'

Macleod nodded. 'That's why they've picked it, nice and easy to get at. His next one, his next one, will be quiet too. He's finding his way. The trouble is, he'll soon start to ramp up. And according to him, he's got a grand finale where people are going to die. Need to get on it, Hope.'

'Just keep Jim off my back. And you're not taking this one over,' she said.

'Not if I can help it,' said Macleod. 'Anyway, I'm off to a press conference. I'm not telling them anything about this stuff.'

'Good idea,' said Hope.

Hope called the team in, sat them down, and then read them the letter.

'Looks legit to me,' said Susan Cunningham, reaching down and almost trying to rub a leg that didn't exist. 'He's seeking attention. He's doing it delicately. He obviously thinks Macleod will be in charge. But he's not that worldly wise, because anybody that knows anything would realise that if somebody didn't die, it wouldn't be Macleod. You'd have to nick something from the arts world for Macleod to even be vaguely involved. He's not that clued up.'

'He's clued enough to hack into a system and blow up a refrigeration plant,' said Ross.

'Well, at least cause a rupture in an ammonia tank,' said Perry.

'Same effect when someone died from it,' said Ross.

'Which he didn't intend,' said Susan. 'I don't know what's driven him over the edge. I don't know if he's an activist, but—'

'What about Jane? Jane was an activist,' said Perry.

'She was indeed. But she seemed quite happy with her company. There's no sign of her even complaining about anything. An activist would turn round and say, "Why can't we do this?" And if the company then didn't do it, they'd maybe take action. She'd know what the risks were; she'd have a good idea about the dangers of letting the ammonia out from a rupture in the tank. She also knew where the shift office was.'

'Unless that was her plan,' said Hope.

'It wasn't,' said Perry. 'She couldn't have known when Derek would be in there. There are too many variables. Shall we release this letter to the public?'

'Cause a panic,' said Hope.

'They're panicked anyway,' said Perry. 'At least this puts a face on it. We might even get people turning around and asking about it. Maybe they'll realise that somebody's upset. They'll have ideas. They'll have—'

'Macleod says no. He thinks it will cause genuine panic.'

'Well, we'd better get on the move with it,' said Perry. 'By the sounds of it, there's going to be another explosion. If it's a rank amateur, somebody doing it for the first time, who's to say they won't end up killing somebody again, even if they don't mean it?'

'And what do they mean by the grand finale,' said Ross. 'He obviously doesn't give that much of a hoot, a school, a pharmacy, could have been kids about there, and a factory, didn't care who was nearby.'

'Depends if he associates them all as being part of it,' said Hope. 'Anyway, we'll see what Jona's come back with. The rest of you, heads down. I want to know the link between those three locations. Ross, you go through the computers, see if they can come up with anything. Perry, Susan, I want the two of you to make sure you go through everything else. All of the witness statements, see if there's any links whatsoever.'

'Will do,' said Susan. 'But I'm telling you now, whatever it is, it's not standing out.'

'No,' said Hope. 'So go find it for me. All of you.'

Chapter 07

Hope made her way down to the forensic labs, having received a call from Jona. The letter that Macleod had received had been taken for analysis. Jona said she had a specialist coming in to speak to her and advised Hope to be there. As Hope walked down, she thought about her team.

Why was everybody so haphazard at the moment, so all over the place? Discombobulated—maybe that was the word. Everyone just didn't seem to be themselves. Even Perry.

'Well, good afternoon to you,' said Jona as Hope entered the forensic labs. 'Over this way; I've got someone you need to meet inside.'

Hope walked over into Jona's office, where a woman was standing looking out of the window.

'Let me introduce Anne Spivak.'

'Hello, Mrs Spivak. I'm DI Hope McGrath.'

'It's Miss, actually, and I know who you are. Seen you on the TV before. Nice to meet you in person.'

'Well, that's all very nice and formal,' said Jona, 'but I've known Anne for a while, so you can take a slightly more relaxed tone, Hope.'

'Okay,' said Hope, 'what have you got for us then?'

'Well,' said Anne, 'Jona found traces of a pollen on the letter, and she brought me in to consult on it. The pollen's quite rare. The flowers are not actually native, but I know that some have been grown. Not in the UK, but only in Scotland, and only on the Isle of Skye.'

'Really?' queried Hope. 'That's very specific.'

'The plant itself isn't indigenous to the UK. It's indigenous to the southern part of Africa. However, it had been brought over for some tests, and I've checked with the site where the flowers are.'

'Where's that?'

'It's a kind of nature garden centre on Skye. They do the usual things of selling teas and coffees to tourists, all that stuff, but they also do a lot of plant research. But the research is quite close.'

'Close to the teas and coffees and everything,' said Hope.

'Well, you kind of walk through the area for the research, so the idea that you could get the pollen picked up is not unreasonable. And then sit down and write your letter.'

'They did this letter in a garden centre?' said Hope. 'Who are we dealing with?'

'Makes you wonder, doesn't it?,' said Jona. 'But that's where it's from, or at least at some point they visited that coffee shop.'

'You know what I'm going to ask, don't you?' said Hope.

'Way ahead of you. I phoned up just to check. No CCTV, no recorded images. It's very much a haphazard sort of thing. They don't get a lot of funding and it's not a place anyone's going to infiltrate and try to steal stuff. It's just somewhere that deals with occasional exotic flowers and sells coffee to tourists.'

'Blast,' said Hope. 'Thank you, Anne,' she said. 'I'd like to say it's been very helpful, but I'm not so sure.'

'We could take somebody down to have a look,' said Jona, 'you know. Let's see if anyone stuck out.'

'Let's see if they remember anybody writing a letter, but we're not even sure when it happened,' said Hope.

'Well, if I find anything else,' said Jona, 'I'll let you know.'

'I'm happy to do some lunch,' said Anne, 'if you wish.'

'I'd love to,' said Hope, 'but I can't really afford the time. We're stuck in the middle of this case and, well . . .'

'I understand,' said Anne.

'Well, I need lunch,' said Jona.

Hope watched the two women disappear. She couldn't very well pop out for lunch when she couldn't even pop home to see John. She met Macleod coming down the stairs as she was climbing back up to the office.

'Think we know where your letter may have been written.'

'You think you may know where it's written. It's not really an awful lot there, is it? What do you know?'

'Don't need to be like that, Seoras,' said Hope. 'It's just that there's a pollen on it. It's a rare pollen, and it's probably come from a plant on the Isle of Skye.'

'We have rare plants on the Isle of Skye that leave their pollen?' asked Macleod.

'No, there's a compact unit there that works on overseas flowers. This one comes from a plant from Southern Africa, but we're unsure where it's exactly been.'

'So, we check the people in the centre.'

'Well, I will do, but it's also right beside a coffee shop. It's a very small centre. Apparently, according to Jona and Anne Spivak, who's the expert, there's potential for cross-contamination into the coffee shop. It's very high.'

'So what you're telling me is, a bomber may have been there, they may have written their letter there, but we haven't got any way of actually working out who they are. CCTV? We could have a row of faces.'

'No CCTV, Seoras. You think in this day and age, but no. I think it's right in the middle of nowhere, this place.'

'Well, get somebody down to interview anyway.'

'Of course,' said Hope. 'Just don't want you getting your hopes up.'

Macleod nodded. Hope continued up to the office and saw Ross sitting at the back. He was looking very morose.

'Have you got a moment, Alan?' Hope shouted.

'Of course,' he said. Ross joined Hope inside her office, and she sat him down at the table to one side where the team usually met for briefings.

'What do you need?' asked Ross.

'I don't need anything. Well, not at the moment. What do you need?'

'What do you mean?'

'You're clearly not happy, Alan. Clearly, it's not suiting you.'

Ross looked at her for a moment and then turned his head away.

'I thought, being a dad, I thought I could get more time. I thought I could be there. Now I am the parent who isn't. Angus is with the wee man every day, playing with him, telling me all these tales. And what am I doing? Hoking my way through video footage, trying to find someone we have no idea about, and starting not to care less about it.'

It was amazingly open for Ross to say so. Maybe that was the trust that Ross had in Hope. She knew he absolutely worshipped Macleod. Thought the man could do no wrong. But Hope was different. Maybe that's why he was allowing himself to be vulnerable with her. Maybe that's why she was able to have time to see him as he was.

'I won't tell you I understand how it is with kids,' said Hope. 'You're the only one on the team with them. You're the only one that has this issue. I'd love to say go home, spend the afternoon, but I can't. You know what it's like. You know the way the press comes down on this and then everybody else jumps. Seoras is making a good fist at the moment of keeping everybody off our backs. But we need to get to solving this.'

'I never asked for a time off. You know I wouldn't. It's not me,' said Ross. 'But something's got to give. Something's got to change. I can't do this. I could when it was just me. Even if it was just me and Angus. Angus can understand. He's able to put aside any angry feelings. He knows I'm a detective. It's what I do. And I do it well.'

'That you do,' said Hope. 'You certainly do it well. But you've been off the boil lately. You haven't been yourself. I thought sending you—'

'You thought sending me to Stornoway to talk to school kids and the like would help. Because what?' asked Ross.

'You'd see children in danger. Children that were put at risk. You'd be able to do something for them. I thought it might—'

'Doesn't work that way. I'm not a big fan of kids,' said Ross. And Hope looked at him, a little bemused.

'Don't get me wrong. I love our kid. I want another one, so he's got a sister. Someone else to grow up with. But I don't like other people's kids. They're messy. Get in the way. They're always not doing what they're told.'

'And yours is an angel?'

'No. But he's mine. And I can deal with it. Somebody else's kids. You're not allowed to deal with it in your own way, got to be careful what Mum or Dad think. You've got to be careful what you say to them. Just can't grab them by the neck either to haul them out of a situation. No. I don't like kids. So you put me in amongst loads of them.'

'Sorry,' said Hope.

'It's okay. I did get some time away, got some time to think. It's hard, you know, when you go home and the little lad's just going off to sleep. Angus gets him all day. And while that causes frustration, because Angus gets upset he doesn't get his own space, what it does do is gives him a great time with him. Angus gets an opportunity to be a dad. I don't. I'm just a guy that pays the bills.'

'Do you want to take time?' asked Hope.

'I wouldn't mind, but I can't.'

'We'll cover it,' said Hope. 'If we have to bring Macleod down. We'll cover it.'

'No, I won't do that,' said Ross. 'I won't leave you in the lurch. When I get rid of this case, we'll be sorted. Then I'll take time.'

'Good,' said Hope. 'Do that.'

Ross stood up and walked over to the door of Hope's office. He stopped and turned, looked at her, smiled, and walked out. That wasn't like him. Certainly not recently. Hope felt she must have got somewhere with him. As she sat there, she looked out and saw Susan and Perry. She walked out to speak to them.

'Perry, Susan. Listen, we've got pollen on the letter that Macleod received. The one talking about the grand finale. Well, turns out that pollen's in Skye. I need you to do a bit of mapping, a bit of identification of what's going on there.

Once you get down to this flower centre, I want you to go through with them, find out if they've got any detail about somebody writing a letter while they were there. They've no CCTV, but—'

'You could send Uniform round to do it,' said Perry.

'No, I want you to do it,' said Hope. 'You two can pull something out of the bag, yes? You'll see something, Perry. You know how to ask people; you know how to talk to them. Scan the irrelevant bits that they say which actually are very relevant.'

'Okay,' said Perry. 'We'll get off now. Probably have to stop the night.'

'Of course. Let's see if you can get me something. Anything. Any route into this person. Too many explosions already. We're just fortunate he doesn't want to actually kill anyone.'

'And we're just unfortunate he already has,' said Perry.

'You know what I mean,' said Hope.

'We'll get on our way,' said Susan.

* * *

'Would you just stick a cigarette in your mouth and smoke it?'

'I don't smoke in the car next to colleagues and I'm quitting. Or I have quit. I haven't had one. You know that.'

'I do know that. It's very obvious,' said Susan.

'Well, I've got to keep going. Sometimes it's worth it.'

'It'll be worth it for you,' said Susan. 'It'll be worth it when you feel better—when you're more lively.'

'Might get some of the weight off as well.'

'Easy, Perry,' said Susan. 'You'd be making yourself into someone I could really fall for.' She laughed. Perry looked across, and then he stopped.

'Oh,' said Susan.

'What?' said Perry.

'You're not yourself. Well, what's the deal?' she asked.

'Well, you know the deal,' said Perry. 'I guess you're the deal.'

'Whoa,' said Susan. There was another hour and a half at least on the drive, and this conversation just got very awkward.

'Look, Perry,' said Susan. 'I like you as a person. I like you as a friend, but I don't feel that way.'

'Okay,' said Perry, crestfallen. He looked towards the ground as much as he could while he was still trying to drive the car.

'It's not that there's anything wrong with you. It's—'

'It's the weight, isn't it? It's the whole overall—'

'Perry—You got me through a lot of this. You saved my life when I was in real trouble. There's a lot I like about you, Perry. I just don't like you in that fashion. I don't like anybody in that fashion at the moment. Please tell me you're not giving up the cigarettes just for me.'

'Not just for you,' he said. 'I could do with losing weight. I could do with getting off the cigarettes, could do with making myself better than I was. You know? I just got into that role. And with the boys, and with drinking after work, and, well, it's a bit different when you suddenly join a team that's half full of women.'

'I guess,' said Susan. 'But one thing you must promise me is everything you do, you do it for you. And I'll help you, the way you've helped me with my leg.'

'Well, it seems to be getting better. Getting to a point where you're going to accept it.'

'No, it's not,' said Susan. 'Perry, I haven't slept in the last four days.'

'Well, you're looking well for it.'

'I'm looking well for it because I've been amongst you lot. I'm looking well because we all look rubbish in the middle of a case, but Perry, trust me when I tell you, I'm exhausted; I'm shot through; I'm shattered. I can feel my leg. In these dreams, I can feel it.'

'So,' said Perry. His hand went over and took Susan's. He squeezed it tightly and then he quickly withdrew his hand.

'It's okay,' said Susan, 'you're trying to comfort me. It's good, I'm okay with that. If you need to, do it. Don't hide away. Okay?' said Susan. 'I've had a bit of a jolt. We stay friends. Maybe you're a bit embarrassed. Don't be. I just don't want anyone at the moment. I'm sorry, Perry. But be my friend. Because I need one at the moment.'

She sat back in the chair, her eyes suddenly gaunt. 'I need one, Perry, because I just lost a very dear and close one.'

Chapter 08

Susan Cunningham lay in her bed at the B&B on the Isle of Skye. They were currently just outside Dunvegan and had a rather quiet dinner. Perry hadn't wanted to talk much following his admission in the car about the feelings he had towards Susan. Susan felt he was being silly. She lay there though.

At three o'clock in the morning, she struggled to get back to sleep. She had awoken an hour earlier. It was another one of the leg nightmares. This time her leg was telling her off for leaving it behind. She couldn't fathom what was going through her head at times. Staying awake in the middle of the night almost seemed more preferable.

They'd gone to the small flower research facility and spoken to those who ran it. But they were struggling to remember anybody who had come through. And certainly anyone coming through who could have picked up that pollen because it was in the walkway into the café.

Susan spun herself off the bed and lifted herself up onto her good leg. She looked around for her crutch, ready to get moving on it. One thing she found was that if she just lay still, she thought too much. Being on the move meant an awful lot less thinking.

She opened her curtains and looked out the window over towards the Minch, the water lying between the mainland and the outer Hebrides. She could see a small lighthouse, the main beam going round and round. The light, once there, then vanishing.

Susan stood on her good leg until she could not stand anymore. She turned and dragged a chair over, hopping all the while, before sitting down on it and looking out.

Her left leg looked strange. It was healing itself from the loss, slowly and surely closing over. It was by far not the most pleasant thing she had seen, but she was getting to some sort of normality. She worked the crutches extremely well, and for that, she was glad.

Susan's ears pricked up. She thought she heard something. She looked out of the window, thinking she had seen a sudden flash. Then again, she was looking out towards the lighthouse, so a sudden flash wouldn't have been that dramatic. Susan was waiting for another flash, just to confirm that the lighthouse was okay. She couldn't remember the exact number of seconds between the first flash and the second, but when it got to thirty seconds, she thought she was definitely missing something. It should have flashed by now, but it wasn't flashing at all.

Susan sighed, and lay back in the chair. She needed to get back to sleep but her mind was racing. She put a phone call through to the Coastguard in Stornoway.

'Hi there,' she said. 'I'm just curious. I'm not interrupting if it's too busy.'

'Busy? It's all routine,' came the reply.

'Good. The lighthouses. Who controls them? Who actually knows what's going on with them?'

'Well, it's the lighthouse board. I can get in touch with them. Why do you want to know?' asked the coastguard.

'I heard something. You see, I'm down on Skye and I'm looking at the lighthouse on the edge of Skye. I heard something and now it doesn't seem to flash.'

'Hold on a minute,' said the coastguard.

Susan Cunningham waited on hold for a moment. She wondered as she waited to be spoken to again if indeed she had been sensible in what she was saying, or was she being laughed at now behind her back?

'Hello,' said the coastguard.

'Hello,' said Susan.

'Well, it's interesting because the Northern Lighthouse Board has just said to me that the light is out. It's just registered a fault, very recently.'

'What are they saying about it?' asked Susan.

'Oh, these things go out all the time? They'll get somebody to examine it, but it might take a day or two.'

'I'm going to take a spin out. Can you give me their number?'

'Okay. Anything we can assist you with? Anything you're worried about?'

'No,' said Susan. 'I just need to have a check to satisfy my curiosity.'

Susan nodded to herself and then placed a call in to the Northern Lighthouse Board.

'Yes, I saw that go out. Was sitting looking at monitoring systems and it disappeared. It's not come back online either. You say the light's gone out?'

'It has indeed. I'm a wee bit of a distance from it, though,' said Susan.

'Okay.'

'Well, I'll get on over and I'll call you,' said Susan. 'Will be a bit. We need to get changed first, though.'

Susan hauled out her cut-up jeans and after changing her underwear and dressing herself in her jeans and t-shirt, she used her crutches to make her way to Perry's room. She knocked on the door but heard snoring beyond. She would just go off herself, drive and have a look, except she couldn't. Susan needed him. She hoped he didn't get too excited as she was turning up in the middle of the night to his room.

Susan continued to knock loudly on the door, and Perry's snoring gradually stopped. He then could be heard moving about before eventually opening the door.

'What's up?' he asked. 'You're changed. What's going on?'

'I think there's just been something going on at one of the lighthouses.'

'One of the lighthouses,' said Perry, his eyes glaring. 'Why are we talking lighthouses?'

'It was there one minute and then it wasn't.'

'You had a nightmare,' said Perry.

'Yes but not about that. We need to go there. Come on.'

'You're not just dreaming this. You didn't nod off and then this came into your head?'

'No, no, it's real,' said Susan.

'People do have full conversations in their dreams, don't they? They bring in people who are—'

'Perry, I've got a missing leg. I'm not dense. I know when I've been dreaming and I know when I'm not. Look, I'm not dreaming this. I've just spoken to the lighthouse board. They say it's gone offline. Let's go have a look. If I'm wrong, we can get back and you can go back to bed.'

'Give me five minutes,' said Perry.

He disappeared back in through the door and Susan stood waiting outside where Perry shortly joined her. She hobbled along on her crutches until she got to the car. Together with Perry, they raced off into the Skye night. As the car wound its way over towards the west side of Skye, Perry mumbled something.

'What?'

'Nothing.'

As the car wound its way along, Susan became more and more anxious about what she thought she had seen. She wasn't daft. She knew something was up.

They went round a corner and then down a track that led to the lighthouse. Susan stopped and looked up at it. There was no flash. No light going off. Well, that clarified what had happened.

'Probably just a power cut,' said Perry.

The two of them got out of the car and walked round the rear side of the lighthouse. There was nothing. Nothing at all. Then they walked round to the other side. Only there did Susan stand and gasp.

'The whole side's blown out. The whole top of that tower's gone. Look. There's glass everywhere on the floor,' said Perry. 'It's an explosion. Why here? Why on earth would you take out up there?'

'I don't know' said Susan. 'I really don't. We're going to have to get people here though.'

'You want to make the calls or do I want to?' asked Perry.

'You do it,' said Susan. 'Just in case I'm dreaming.'

Perry threw her a look, then wandered off to call colleagues and other services about what had happened.

Susan sat down on a rock. Her head was racing with

thoughts. Four explosions. A lighthouse. What did that have to do with the others? There was a local pharmacy. There was a primary school. And then there was a frozen food processing plant. Why on earth would you be bothered by all this? Why on earth would you be targeting these people?

None of the companies made sense. This wasn't even a company; this was a lighthouse board. This was something that was there simply to protect people. Was that the clue? Were they after things that protected people? But why? Why on earth? And it wouldn't stop people in their tracks. Ships would still sail despite this being out. They'd be advised that the lighthouse wasn't there, that there was no light. But it wouldn't stop them from sailing. Nowadays, things are so much more automated. GPS systems that helped ships run along plotted courses.

It took all night and into the following morning to get a forensic team down to have a look around the site. In truth, it was pretty obvious what had happened. The door at the bottom had been opened. It had an alarm on it, but the alarm had been bypassed. Whoever had done it had at least a reasonable knowledge of security systems. Susan called Hope that morning.

'We're just gathering together,' said Hope. 'Well, those of us who are still here; stick your phone on. Join in the call.' Susan called Perry over and soon Perry and she were sitting a little distance off in their car. Her phone showed a screen of Hope, Jona and Ross, along with Macleod and a side screen of Perry and Susan.

'I've been looking,' said Ross, 'and there seems to be a connection here.'

'What do you mean, a connection?' asked Hope.

'Funding applications. I'm getting funding applications for all of these.'

'Funding applications? So what? A pharmacy can make funding applications?' said Hope.

'Well, the funding applications, they aren't made by anyone. The thing is, the buildings in the applications were old and have been restored, such as the pharmacy, or it's a school. It's a worthy cause.'

'What about the food factory?' asked Macleod.

'That got financial help because the building it was in had been old and it had to be reclad.'

'And on Skye?' asked Hope.

'That lighthouse has had funding to maintain it.'

'So what?' said Hope. 'We've got a bomber who is keen to make sure that funding and application money is sent to better places.'

'It's good, Ross,' said Macleod. 'You need to keep on that.'

'Well, that's the only thing we've got,' said Hope. 'And we know our bomber must have been there not that long ago. You need to go back to the flower place and see if you can get any idea of who's been through in the recent couple of days.'

'Will do,' said Susan.

'One thing I don't get,' said Macleod. 'Why this? Why so small scale? Is it just put up to say that this is what's happening. And there's a grand finale. This doesn't build it, does it? This is—'

'Maybe this is part of the message,' said Perry.

'In what way?' That's the only thing we've got,' asked Hope.

'I don't know. I'm not saying that it is. What I'm saying is, maybe it is.'

'You're going to have to do better than that for me, Perry,' said Hope.

'Well, is there anything about where these things are happening?' asked Perry.

'How do you mean?'

'Well, when we plot them, do we see anything? When you look at the towns and the villages they're in, does it mean anything?' asked Perry.

'I don't know,' said Hope. 'The good news is, is that we've got something to go on after having nothing. So, pull them together; look at these funding applications; let's check who's been involved with them, who made them, who agreed to them. Was anybody else putting in for other funding operations? Maybe for a hospital, maybe for a community centre, something where people will get snubbed.'

'I don't see how that fits,' said Ross.

'It fits,' said Perry, 'because you would blow something up to get the attention. You don't look to kill.'

'Except somebody got killed in the first one,' said Susan. 'Why wouldn't you stop then if that was your case?'

'You've got to believe in the cause. You're telling yourself,' said Perry, 'that this was an accident. Accidents happen.'

'What do you mean?' asked Macleod.

'I just said that accidents happen.' Perry was suddenly looking out the car window.

'You all right?' asked Susan.

'I'm fine,' said Perry. 'I just don't know what that means.'

'Thank you, everyone,' said Hope and closed down the call. Perry went to get back out of the car, but Susan stopped him.

'You okay?'

'Yes,' said Perry. 'Why shouldn't I be?'

'You know why not. I know the feelings you're feeling, but

it's—'

'It's blooming awkward to talk about them,' said Perry. 'Blooming awkward.' He got out of the car and walked over to one of the local officers. Susan heard the tone straight away.

'Can I borrow DC Perry for a minute?' said Susan, out of the car.

Perry came over. He went to help her up, but she stopped trying to get out of the car for a moment.

'So you're annoyed. You're pissed at me. Don't take it out on them.'

'I'm not annoyed with you. I'm just disappointed.'

'Perry. You're a sweet man. You're a very sweet man. If I was interested in anyone, yes, it might even be you.'

'You have no idea how that is the last thing I want to hear. Do you need a hand out or not?'

Susan didn't. But she said she did, so he lifted her up onto her feet.

She wondered, would this desire of his cool, or would working together just not be the thing anymore? She needed him, though. He was helping her. He was good for her. Regarding her missing leg, he'd been the third crutch. She didn't want that to go away. She didn't want him to go away.

Chapter 09

'I think we need another go at Solace,' said Hope. 'I know she said that she had nothing to do with it, but given what was on her laptop, I think there's something there. She's holding something back.'

'Maybe,' said Ross.

'Just maybe.'

'Well, we got into all her systems.'

'Have you not got a more considered opinion than that?' asked Hope. Ross looked the other way. 'Get her in. We need to interview her again.'

'It'll take a few hours to bring her up this way.'

'That's fine,' said Hope. 'Get them to bring her up. We'll sit down together, okay?'

'Okay,' said Ross.

Ross left the room, and Hope blew out to the air. This felt like she was treading through treacle with everyone. It didn't feel like a dynamic team. Macleod never had a team that felt like they were in treacle. Macleod always had them on the punch. Always on the ball.

No, that wasn't true, was it? There were times he struggled. She needed to stop berating herself.

Hope turned and looked out the window. She could see why Macleod had enjoyed this window. He never saw all the press from it, unlike his current office.

The telephone rang, and Hope spun, picking it up.

'So what sort of day is it?' asked John, her partner.

'Thanks for ringing,' she said.

'What's up?' asked John.

'Oh, it's just feeling like, well, it feels like I'm wading through treacle, if I'm honest. Everybody's just so lacklustre, so—'

'Well, chivvy them up then,' said John.

'I know, but I'm lacklustre, too.'

'That's not what I wanted to hear,' said John. 'Any chance of getting—'

'No,' said Hope. 'None.'

There was a silence then across the phone, broken eventually by John. 'Well, let's hope you get to the bottom of this case soon then, because I think both of us are—'

'You don't have to tell me,' interrupted Hope. 'I know where I want to be, and it's with you, doing some fun things. But I'm here, we're stuck, and I have to get on with it.'

'Do you want me to bring you lunch in? Or to—'

'Yes,' said Hope. 'Bring me lunch.'

'I'll see you in about half an hour,' said John.

Hope smiled as she put the phone down. It wasn't what they both wanted, but, hey, it was lunch. She strode out into the main office, where Perry and Susan were working hard on the explosion sites.

'Are we finding anything, then?' asked Hope.

'Well, they have all asked for funding, but I'm struggling to see what the connection with that is. The funding's general funding. It's done by a trust that's looking after

Scotland. There's nothing untoward in it. I can't even find anything wrong with the people who are putting up the money. Everything seems to be up legitimate. All backed by the government. Yes, there's advertising and applications but, you know, it all seems perfectly okay.'

'What about you, Susan?' asked Hope. She saw Susan look up rather sheepishly. 'You okay?'

'No.' Susan looked away.

'Something I need to know about.'

'She's having a—well, she's still missing her leg,' said Perry. 'Emotionally.'

'And physically,' said Susan. 'I just . . . well . . . it's just gone. I don't think you'll get it.'

'Maybe not,' said Hope. 'Do you want me to book you in with a counsellor? Make contact with them?'

'I've already made contact. Perry's looking after me.'

Hope watched as Perry nodded, but his eyes were over towards Susan.

'I'm bringing in Solace again. Going to give it a go, but Ross is going to do it with me. You two keep going. See if we can find any more links. I need to have something to give Macleod when he turns up. I think he's off on another press conference.'

'Papers are saying—' started Perry.

'I don't care what the papers say,' said Hope. 'I'm having lunch with John in my office. I don't want to be disturbed unless you have to.'

'Of course,' said Perry. Hope made her way back into the office and sat down to do some paperwork. Approximately ten minutes later, there was a knock at the door. She shouted, 'Come in,' and smiled as John almost bounded into the office.

'Chicken salad—is that okay? I think it's the one you like.

Honey mustard dressing.'

'Come over here,' said Hope. John bounded round to Hope's side of the desk and sat down on her lap. She gave him a kiss.

'How's the world of car hire going?' she asked.

'You don't want to know about the worst customer ever today.'

'I do want to know,' said Hope. 'I want you to talk to me about anything but police work, about explosions. Talk about anything else.'

'Well, she comes in and she's got this kid and the kid is a pain,' said John.

He continued with his tale for the next ten minutes and Hope smiled. She wasn't really listening, but it was taking her mind off things. She sat down with him, eating her lunch and then, when it was time for him to go, she stood and held him, kissing and hugging tight. She could feel the excitement and disappointment in him.

'We will get time,' said Hope. 'It's just—'

'I know,' said John. 'I know. Are you okay, though?'

'You know,' said Hope. 'It's just—well, Alan's up to high dough. Warren's off the cigs and jittery at times. And Susan's—well, Susan's lost her leg. She's doing great, but I think it's hitting her.'

'Keep going,' said John. 'Be as wonderful as you are.'

Hope smiled. He always lifted her, was always there, just what she needed. He turned to walk out of the office, and she reached for him, pulling him back in close from behind, hugging him.

'I got to go,' he said. 'And besides, you just get me thinking of things that are going to happen that aren't.'

'They are going to happen,' said Hope. 'They're not happening right now, but they're going to happen—trust me.'

'You know I do,' he said as he walked out the door. 'Besides, you can't leave this body alone.'

He said it out loud into the office, causing a few looks. Hope laughed. That was his intent. She went back to her work, and shortly after, Ross arrived.

'That's Solace downstairs,' he said. He turned to go before Hope had even stood up.

'Are you ready for this?' she asked him.

'What's the line of attack?'

'Withholding information. She's got something else on the go. She must have.'

They walked down together but Hope felt like Ross was a million miles away. When he entered the interview room, he sat down but he was slouched. Not his usual self, prim and proper Ross.

Hope started the recording software and gave the warnings, explanations, and introductions. And then looked across at Jean Solace who was staring back at her.

'We have gone through all your computer records?'

'Yes, you told me.'

'And you've been on different incendiary sites. You've got an activist background. We've got explosions going off with nobody getting killed except for that first one. Which makes me think it was an accident. What is it you're trying to prove?'

'I'm not trying to prove anything,' she said. 'I don't know how people got my password, or into my connection.'

'Did you write it down anywhere?' asked Hope.

'No.'

'Did anybody look over your shoulder when you were putting it in?'

'I don't know.'

'Whoever is found to have done this, you realise that it's one step off murder.'

'It wasn't me,' she said.

'DC Ross here, went through all your records. He says you've got form for being an activist, and the activism is amongst groups that would carry out this type of work. Isn't that right, DC Ross?'

There was silence beside Hope.

'DC Ross,' she said again.

'Yeah,' said Ross. 'That's correct.'

Hope wanted to stare at him, but that would give the initiative over to Jane Solace and she wanted to round on her now.

'Of course, it may not have been you. It may have been one of your group. It may have all got out of hand. After all,—'

'Nothing's got out of hand,' said Jane. 'Absolutely nothing.'

'Really? Would you say the crime sites were likely targets for the groups that Jane subscribes to?' Hope asked Ross.

There was silence again. Hope could feel the anger building up inside her, but she tried to stay focused. 'DC Ross,' she said. 'Would you say so?'

'Absolutely,' said Ross, suddenly.

'Maybe it's not something you chose to do. Maybe it's something you were led into. I have to warn you that if somebody's coerced you into something and you don't admit it, and then it turns out that it's all been part of a plot to kill or to destroy, you could be implicated as well. And in a serious way. We have a death on our hands.'

'Okay,' she said. 'I don't want to go down for anything. I don't want to be told that.'

'Be told what?' asked Hope.

'That what I did caused somebody's death. I didn't think anything would come of it.'

'Come of what?'

'The thing is, well, one of these groups I belong to. I went to one of their meetings once. Stayed over and, well, had quite a lot of drinks. I was young back then. Photographs were taken of me in compromising positions.'

'Can you confirm this?' said Hope.

'They sent me the photographs recently. Told me they wanted the password for the system. It's a system for a frozen food plant. That's why I gave it away. And then when it exploded, I didn't know what to do. After all, well, Derek died, didn't he?'

Jane's eyes welled up. She leaned forward, a hand bracing herself on the table.

'Who are they? The people with this photograph.'

'That's the thing. I don't know. I truly don't know. It wasn't the main group.'

'Do any of them know?'

'I contacted my group. I tried to do it on the quiet, but they're unaware of who this other group were as well. They were a separate group that came in.'

'Where did they come in from? A different part of the country?'

'I don't know. I don't know what I told them. I don't know anything about them. All I know is they've got photographs.'

'We'll need them,' said Hope. 'We'll need to see if we can trace them back.'

'Dear God, it killed Derek. They killed Derek with it. I was friends with Derek. Derek was the closest thing I had to a buddy in there.'

'Why would these people want to blow up the frozen food factory? Or cause such damage? What line of activism were they in?'

'That's the thing. It's animal rights I'm into. It's got nothing to do with a frozen food company. It's doing frozen veg. It's animal rights. We don't kill any animals. We don't do anything like that. And yet they insisted on having them. I thought they were just going to put a virus in it, cause it to slow down. I mean, the company does other frozen food products, but even then, it's bits of a chicken.

'We don't actually grow the chickens. We don't kill them. We don't make them fat. We get all the meat in frozen. Somebody else does all that. It makes no sense.'

She twisted in her seat, looking off to one side, tears falling from her face.

'Anything else to add, DC Ross?'

'No,' mumbled Ross.

'I'll halt the interview there, then,' said Hope. She called for a constable to come into the room, and asked her to sort out Jane. She advised a cup of tea, saying she'd come back later to tidy things up. But as she left the interview room, Ross followed, until they got down to the end of the corridor, at which point she turned on him.

'What the hell's that?' asked Hope.

'What do you mean?' asked Ross.

'You're not even in there with me. Just not in there. You need to get your head back in it. Okay? You're having issues; you're having problems. So are we all. But you've got to get your head in it, or you've got to declare yourself unfit and get out of my team. Because at the moment, we're carrying you. I could have had Perry in there. But no, I said I'd give my sergeant his due and he can come in with me. But you treat me like that.'

'It's just too long. Just the hours. Just everything.'

'But get with it, Alan,' said Hope. He gave a half nod and walked off. But Hope wasn't sure if he'd really taken it in.

Interesting, though, about Solace, she thought. Who would have the ability to find out what she'd done before? Who were these people that she'd clearly cavorted with and got caught out by? There weren't many leads in this case. But she told herself she was prising one open at the moment and that she'd have to keep going.

Chapter 10

Hope McGrath was feeling in a better mood. She'd woken up at three in the morning, her mind racing about her team. She thought of Ross just not being himself, of Susan struggling, and then of Perry trying to console her. The poor man trying to draw closer with no luck. Hope wondered just whether she was cut out to handle them all. She'd gone over from the bed to the window, pulling the curtains back only a touch. As she never wore much in bed, and the streetlights often lit up her window, she feared getting caught out by some drunken person returning home.

The street, however, was empty. She stood and looked at it. She wished she could have just two weeks away. Two weeks somewhere else. She heard John get up behind her and felt his hands. And after that, they had fallen into what could be described as the best two hours of the last week.

Later, when Hope arrived at work, she felt somewhat tired, but she was happy. As she stood in her office, the most depressing thing about it all was that she'd skipped up the steps to the floor her office was on. Macleod had been coming down the other direction. He'd smiled at her and simply said nothing. He usually would have given her at least a good morning or a 'how's it going,' some sort of check-in. Instead, he just smiled.

She arrived before the team and drew out a map, marking the explosion sites. As she did so, she saw something in it. She drew lines from one to the other, first from this one to that one, then from another one, pulling them back together again. She was seeing a symbol in it. And she wondered what it was. Could it be an H? She wasn't sure. She extended one leg of what would have been an H.

Drawing it down further, Hope realised that the line ran through several places, one of them being Ullapool.

Why would you want to put a bomb somewhere in Ullapool? she thought. *Why would you want to blow up a lighthouse in Skye? Maybe*, she thought. *Maybe if they could take a look to see if anywhere in Ullapool had received funding.*

The team started to arrive, gathering in the outer office. Hope strode out, calling them in, and then stood proudly in front of her map, which was pinned on a board.

'What's happening, boss?' asked Perry as he came in through the door. He had one hand almost ready to catch Susan Cunningham who was hobbling in on her crutches. Her face looked tired and worn. No wonder if she'd not been sleeping.

'Right, I've been looking at possible symbols. I've drawn out the map of the explosion sites. If you connect the dots, you could get an H.'

So, what?' asked Susan. 'We're thinking our next attack is going to be where?'

'Well, I don't know,' said Hope. 'If you extend the shape, Ullapool's on that line. That's the only major sort of town. There are a few other smaller places. I want you to see if anywhere in Ullapool's had funding. Okay. And if they have, maybe we'll head out that way. See if there's a connection between them and the other sites.'

Will do,' said Perry.

'I'll take this up to Macleod. He needs to see we're actually going forward somewhere.'

'Well, maybe wait until we have something concrete,' said Ross.

'You just think this is a coincidence?' asked Hope.

'We do not know if it is or not, yet.'

Hope left the team to get on with it and walked up the stairs to Macleod's office. She waved over at the secretary, who simply waved her in, showing that Macleod would not be busy. She rapped the door, heard a 'Come in' and stepped inside to see Clarissa Urquhart sitting in front of Macleod's desk.

He always called Hope in if Clarissa was sitting there. She loved Clarissa. She was a good colleague, but if he saw things differently to Clarissa, she could lay it on thick. No doubt she was giving Macleod grief about when the budgets weren't enough to do what he wanted her to do. They'd be brought up and anything else that was annoying her in the world.

'Do you know he always does this?'

'Does what?' asked Hope.

'Any time I talk to him about what I need and that door goes, he just calls people in. You don't get, "Wait a minute"; you don't get "What's going on". All you get is him pulling somebody else in, hoping I forget what the conversation is.'

'But while you're here,' said Hope, walking over to draw a symbol on the board, which represented what she'd drawn on the map downstairs.

'What's that?' asked Macleod.

'It's a really poorly drawn H,' said Clarissa.

'Cheers, Clarissa,' said Hope. 'What is it? It's got to represent a symbol from somewhere. It must—'

'Why?' asked Macleod.

'Because that's where the bomber's planted everything. In that shape.'

'Is that the end shape, though?' asked Clarissa. 'Is there more to come?'

'I think there's more to come.'

Meanwhile, Macleod was on his feet, walking round past Clarissa, towards the maps.

'It does look like something,' said Macleod; 'can you put it on the map? Where does it show?'

'We don't know because we don't know the length of the legs. But it does run a line through Ullapool.'

'Why Ullapool?' said Macleod. 'Why are these places so far away? Have you checked to see if anyone's got funding in Ullapool? The rest had.'

'Looking it up at the moment. I thought I'd bring you up to date.'

'It's not an ancient symbol,' said Clarissa. 'At least none I'm familiar with, and I know quite a lot of them.'

'So basically, you're asking if this is a symbol of sorts,' said Macleod. 'I don't know, it may even be a simpler symbol. Don't overcomplicate it. Get everybody in the books. Get everybody online; see if they can work out what it is.'

'Okay,' said Hope.

'Remember, it may be ancient,' said Macleod. 'We do not know why this person's doing this. Therefore, take everything as a possibility.'

Hope nodded, thanked Clarissa, and disappeared from the room as she made her way back down the stairs. There was still that same spring in her step.

When Hope returned to the office, she was stunned to see that Ross was working away, not just diligently but almost with a passion. Perry was standing behind him, looking bemused at the computer screen while Susan Cunningham was on her own.

'Did you find anything?'

'You don't know how many symbols there are in this world. We are getting there by all means.'

'Keep me informed,' said Hope, disappearing back into her office. She was looking to clean out more paperwork, but then she heard a scream from the other office. She ran out.

'What's going on?'

Susan Cunningham was sitting in Perry's arms, crying into his shoulder.

'Are you all right?' asked Hope.

'Just a nightmare. I nodded off for a moment and then suddenly, it wasn't there. Suddenly, it was.'

'Take the rest of the day if you need it,' said Hope.

'I can't,' she said. 'I've got to keep it together; keep doing it for all those other people.'

'You don't have to do it for anyone,' said Hope. 'There are always plenty of people who can come in and help out.'

Hope continued with some more paperwork, but her mind was on the case.

She kept looking up at the map, at the legs she'd drawn. Legs for what? How are the legs important? Were there any symbols that were an extended H with legs? The only one she knew was a helicopter landing pad, and it would have to be a blooming big helicopter to land on this one. She stood up, walked to the window again, then she walked back.

'Got to be somewhere,' she said out loud. 'Gotta be something about it.'

She didn't like to pester the team. But now she walked out in front of them all, waving her hands to get everyone to stop.

'Update report. Anyone?'

'There's nothing. Nothing from anyone.' Ross was clearly worked up, but he was doing what he was good at.

Hope wondered just how long it would take as well before the next bomb attack. Jona came into the office to check in.

'Get anything else more for me?' Hope asked.

'No. All the explosives could be put together easily. You'd have to know what you were doing, but you could buy the parts from here, there, and everywhere. We will not get a break like we did with the letter.'

'You think the letter's real?'

'It's very real,' said Jona. 'Completely real.'

Hope felt like she was on the way to something with her H symbol, but she was struggling because no one else seemed to believe in it. But it was more than that bothering her. Ross was indifferent to her situation. He was enjoying himself in the task he'd been given. Sitting in front of his computer brought him more joy than anything else.

'Hope, I might have something later on this afternoon. I've got a hold of all the funding applications. I'm going to have to go into them and try to see if I can cross reference stuff, see if anything matches with your "H-plan" theory.'

Ross put his head back down to his computer and Hope walked back into her office. She was feeling more and more on edge, wanting the case to break. There were days like this when it just didn't happen. Days you wished would run quicker.

Hope sat back in her chair. She had done what she could with the note. She'd gone out and looked for people to help her. They were clutching at straws with this pattern idea but there was so little to go on.

Hope had been feeling the strain. So when John had suggested that morning he give her a rub down, she had taken him up on that offer. In fairness to him, he was good at it. But the worries and the strain didn't go away. Maybe she'd get home tonight. Maybe she wouldn't. But she wanted to go back to this morning, and her time with John. Now.

Hope stood, hands in jeans, staring again at the map again. It was an H, wasn't it? What else was going? Was anywhere else going to be involved? Time would tell.

Chapter 11

Perry started banging on the door of Hope's office excitedly.

'Come in. Hurry and come in,' she said. He burst through the door. 'What is it?' asked Hope.

'I've got it. There are three places in Ullapool that have had this sort of funding. Two of them quite small. There's one that used to be an old shop. There's another one that's actually a piece of wall. And the third one is a church.'

'Okay,' said Hope. 'And what's the connection between them all?'

'I don't know, apart from them being on the funding list,' said Perry. 'I was thinking we might go there.'

'Who's going?' asked Hope.

'Well, I could take Susan with me.'

'I think we want to go to Ross first. See if he wants to make a trip across.'

Perry turned to go back out, but he was almost clattered by Ross working his way into the office.

'Hope,' he said, 'we need to go to Ullapool.'

'So Perry says.'

Ross looked at him. 'How did you know?'

'Because I've done the legwork.' said Perry. 'We've got a wall, we've got a shop, and then we've got a church that have all had funding from the—'

'No, no, no,' said Ross, 'new explosion.'

'What explosion?' blurted Perry.

'That's why I'm running. There's been an explosion, and it's in a church in Ullapool.'

'We need to go then,' said Hope; 'all four of us. I'll see you downstairs,' she said to Perry. 'You can drive my car. Ross, take Susan.'

'I don't mind taking Susan,' said Perry.

'Well, I do mind you taking her, because I want to pick your brains in the way over. I don't want Ross driving alone.'

Ross just shook his shoulders, and disappeared off into the office.

'Two minutes, Perry. I'll see you downstairs,' said Hope.

Two minutes later, Perry jumped into Hope's car, took the keys from Hope, and turned on the ignition. Before he reversed the car, he looked out the window to see Susan Cunningham scooting to Ross's car with her crutches.

'She'll be all right,' said Hope. 'You don't need to—'

'What?' said Perry. 'Help her? I think I do. I've been getting her on the move. She's been getting down lately. And who can blame her? After all, not everybody ends up losing a leg. But I think she's doing tremendously well.'

'She was doing tremendously well,' said Hope. 'There seems to be—'

'She's getting nightmares. Even outside of work hours. You're not seeing the half of it.'

'I'm sorry? I'm not seeing the half of what?' asked Hope.

'When I drop her off at home at night, and then pick her

up in the morning, you can see it. She's not sleeping right. She's—'

'Perry, do you think sometimes you're too close?'

The question jarred Perry. It took him a moment to come back with any sort of answer.

'Too close?' he said. 'How can I be too close? How can—'

'She's very needy at the moment because of all these things. I know you're wanting to help her. And, well, some people have said you might want a bit more, which is not really any of my business, unless it affects the team. I need you more detached. You seem to be more about helping Susan to continue with her job and not sorting out your own.'

'Have we been slacking with anything?' he asked.

'No, you haven't. But you're not being Perry. I need your mind open. I need you looking at all the possibilities to tell me what's going on. Because that's what you're good at, seeing what's hidden behind everything else.'

'Caring for a colleague doesn't do that.'

'It's more than care, Perry. I think we can all see that,' snapped Hope.

Perry didn't quite blush, but he certainly seemed to withdraw into the seat. Perry was a large-enough figure, but just right now he seemed like he was a twelve-year-old boy.

'I'll deal with it,' he said.

'Don't be like that, Perry,' said Hope. 'We've all got things going on; we've all got difficulties, okay? You're seeing that Ross is struggling at the moment; everyone's seeing that. I'm struggling.'

'How are you struggling?' asked Perry. 'You came in this morning, you found that map, you were buzzing. You were—'

'Still struggling, Perry. Trying to get time for other people.

It's difficult.'

'No, it's not,' said Perry. That seemed to end the discussion.

Hope sat in silence as the car raced on along the single carriageway over to Ullapool. When they arrived at the church, Hope wondered at first if they'd found the right place. There was a police constable standing nearby, which was the only thing that indicated anything was wrong.

'Hello, constable. I'm DI Hope McGrath.'

'I know who you are,' said the constable. 'We all know who you are. Even my kids know you from the telly. All the press conferences. You don't seem to be doing those anymore.'

The constable is quite chatty, thought Hope. *Not quite inappropriately so but getting to that way.*

'The DCI is covering that off at the moment. So what's the story here?'

'Window blown out on the left-hand side of the building. Careful, there's glass round there. I believe the forensic team is on their way.'

Of course, thought Hope. They called in Jona. Ross pulled up in his car along with Susan Cunningham who then got out of the car. She began to hop along.

Perry instinctively moved towards her, then Hope saw him pull away and move over towards her.

'What would you like us to look at, Detective Inspector?' he asked.

'Perry, go inside the church. Get some details about it. See when and where the restoration work was done.'

'Will do.' He took off, leaving Susan Cunningham to approach Hope on her own.

'What about me?' she asked.

'Start doing a canvas of the area if you can. Very nearby. The houses that overlook it. See if anyone has seen anything.'

Ross began to chat to the constable and then turned to Hope. 'I'll get some statements done from people who heard the explosion.'

'Good,' said Hope. 'No one's injured, again,' she said to Ross. 'If it hadn't had been for that first incident, we wouldn't be involved.'

'No, we wouldn't,' said Ross, 'and I'd be at home.'

'You're not wrong there,' said Hope. *And I'd be getting bed time,* Hope thought to herself. A wry smile came across her face, which made the constable looking at her wonder what was going on. But he never asked.

Hope toured the church and found minor damage until Perry came up to her.

'The window was blown out. Stained glass around it. Apparently when they did the work, they had to fix a lot of the mortar and the stonework around the edges. It's quite a custom job in some ways.'

'And who did it?'

'Well,' Perry said, 'it's all organised by the same trust. So, they don't know. Workmen turned up, workmen did, workmen left. Nobody here seems to know who they actually were. They just said they were from the trust handing out the money.'

Hope nodded, then saw Susan Cunningham being helped along by Perry again. She glanced over at him, but he gave her a hard stare back. She caught up with him a few minutes later.

'She just needed a hand. It's another episode. It's like more of a flashback. And then she just doesn't feel right.'

Ross came across to talk to Hope. 'They're very upset here,' he said. 'Apparently that window's quite something. It's been in the church for over one hundred and fifty years. A lot of money was put into fixing it and now somebody's just blown it apart.'

'Who?' asked Hope.

'Well, the locals are saying it's vandals.'

'Explosion by vandals? Vandals would put a brick through it,' said Hope. 'This is our person again.'

'Got something,' said Susan Cunningham. She was on the floor beneath a pew of the church.

'What have you got?'

'That's a letter,' she said. Hope noticed that Susan's hands were gloved as she read it. '"The forgotten will rise." That's all it says. The handwriting looks similar to the one that the boss received, though.'

'Okay,' said Hope. 'You need to get that letter to Jona. Perry, Ross, the forgotten will rise. Any ideas?'

'Give me a minute,' said Ross. He pulled out his laptop.

'He's blowing all these places up, which you would think would leave a big clue. He seems to use the same explosive, except for that first time. Nobody's getting hurt and yet he's making a point. A point that we haven't been told what it is yet. This is the first statement towards it. "The forgotten will rise." But it's so generic, it's useless.

'Ross, start looking into campaigns. See if that slogan's ever used.'

'Not found anything so far,' said Ross. 'I'm way ahead of you on that one but let's see if we can dig anything more about it.'

Hope stepped outside, and breathed in the sea air. That was the nice thing about Ullapool. You had the sea round about you here, and often the wind was cut out by the houses and the sun would shine down upon you. She looked out, wondering when the ferry would come round the corner. A daily event for the locals, excitement for the tourists. As she stood there, she was approached by a woman in a collar.

'Hello,' said Hope. 'I'm DCI Hope McGrath.'

'I'm Reverend Allison McGinley. I had an idea that someone would do this. We had trouble with vandals,' she said, 'but somebody told me this was an explosion. Not a—'

'That's right. The glass is all blown out. Not come from the outside, the explosions come from the inside. It's very similar to other explosions we've been having. You may have heard about them in the news.'

'It's a pain,' she said. 'We haven't long had that window done. It was falling into disrepair and the Trust came along and said they would help us. It looked great. Now, I don't know where this leaves us. I don't know if the insurance covers a bomb.'

'I'm afraid I can't help you with that. There's no one holding a grudge?' asked Hope.

'No,' said the minister.

'What about the Trust? Did they put any special requests around the window? Did the people who came to do it do a good job?'

'They weren't from here, weren't local. That's the way of things nowadays, isn't it? I think they might have got a lot of the Trust work.'

'Did they do any of the others?'

'The wall was done by somebody different because it was a dry stonewall building that they wanted. So, they had to get specialists in for that. The other building, it was done slightly earlier. I don't think it was the same people.'

That's interesting, thought Hope. *It's somebody different who builds and yet this one gets blown up*. She wondered if that was something else to look at. One thing she considered was that the note wasn't much of a clue.

There was talk of a major ending to all of this. They'd been told after all that the explosions would culminate in a grand finale. There'd been talk of deaths and yet everything coming up to this wasn't. It was just one down so far as a murder investigation was concerned.

Hope wondered just what was the person at? Was this practice? They'd had that before. Somebody had practiced. She remembered that in an earlier case with Macleod. Someone had tried out different ways of killing people. Was this a practice run of bombings?

As she stood there, someone walked up to her. 'You run this case, don't you?'

'May I ask who you are?'

'I'm Moira. And I'm not happy. How am I going to go about my business? How am I meant to do things when this is all happening? You should start looking at this more closely.'

'I'm standing in this spot looking at the broken window,' spat Hope. 'How close do you want me to get?'

'That's the trouble with you people. You're just there to do your jobs. Just take your pay and go.'

Hope was going to rise to the bait. But she didn't, instead, relaxing. 'Would you kindly move on?' asked Hope.

As the woman left, Hope began to question what was really going on. Maybe she needed to look at this more obtusely. Maybe she needed to hunt things down differently. She'd have to get on to looking more closely at what was happening with the money and the funding. Were there stories in there? Who knew?

In the meantime, she needed to be getting back to the office.

Chapter 12

Macleod sat in his office wondering how the team down below were getting on. He was busy signing more paperwork. He had a senior meeting later on that afternoon and he also at some point had to pop out and get Jane a birthday present. Macleod didn't enjoy buying birthday presents because he was just rubbish at picking what people liked.

She didn't love him because he showered with gifts; she loved him because she got on with him and he was one with her, or so he thought. Jane teased him about gifts but she also said it didn't matter. But Macleod thought it should matter. He would not be one of these people who just got their secretary to pick stuff out. He would pick it out and then Jane could either like it or lump it. It was the thought that counted after all.

He had told her that, two years previously, with the matching set of egg cups. Jane gave him a look that asked how much thought was put into this then. And since that day, Macleod had decided he needed to make a bit more of an effort.

He'd allowed himself two hours of shopping. For a man who never shopped, this was looking like it was going to be an interminable time. There was a knock at the door and his secretary stepped in.

'Post, Seoras,' she said.

'Put it on the table in the inbox,' he said. 'I'm disappearing this afternoon. Don't forget that.'

'It's in your diary; I put it in. I certainly won't forget it,' she said.

'No, you won't. I might,' he said. 'So, I'm really telling you to make sure that I remember.'

'That is my job.'

Macleod smiled at the woman as she left, before reaching forward for the letters. He picked up the first one. It was from a local counsellor, and it would be a whine about something. He promptly placed it back down. There was one in the brown envelope, and he thought he recognised the handwriting. He donned a pair of latex gloves before opening the letter.

He laid it out on the table in front of him and knew he was right. 'Next time,' said the letter, 'there will be a boom at the home of Dumpher's flat tune.'

This is different, thought Macleod. It actually said something. It was yanking your chain.

He picked up the phone and called Hope. She was on her way back from Ullapool, the team following behind. When Hope arrived half an hour later, Macleod had taken a photo of the letter down to Hope's office. He was sitting waiting for her as she walked in.

'I keep telling you, if you like it that much, you can move back in.'

'It doesn't come with a secretary, so you can keep it.' He smiled.

'Oh, what's up with this letter, then?' she said. 'Does it say any more?'

'There's going to be a bomb at the home of Dumpher's flat tune.'

'What?' said Hope. 'That's it?'

'That's it,' said Macleod. 'It must be done by somebody from Crossword Puzzle police.'

'Who on earth is Dumpher?'

'I don't know,' said Macleod. 'I don't know at all.'

Perry marched in, their car making up time behind her quicker than she would have liked. 'What have we got?'

'Dumpher's flat tune. Where's the home of Dumpher's flat tune, Perry?'

'For goodness' sake,' said Perry. He turned and marched out of the office.

'Is he okay?' asked Macleod.

'You know he's off the cigs.'

'It doesn't seem to be affecting him then,' said Macleod. 'Blimey, not by half.'

Susan Cunningham came hopping in behind. 'Home of Dumpher's flat tune, Susan. Where is it?'

'Don't know.'

Meanwhile, Ross hadn't come in. Hope looked around and saw he was on the phone at his desk. She went to the door, looked round to wave him in, but his face was pale.

'Alan' shouted Hope from her office door. 'What's happening? What's up?'

'The wee man's not well. He's struggling. Struggling with his breathing. Something . . . something's not right.'

'Go!' said Hope.

'We're working. I can—'

'Go,' said Hope. 'It's not an offer; it's not a request; it's an order. Go!'

Ross looked up at her, turned, walked over to the coat stand that he'd just recently thrown his coat onto and raced out the door.

'Where's he going?' asked Macleod from inside Hope's office.

'Child's not well. Told him to go.'

'Just right. But how are we going to find out about the home of Dumpher's flat tune?' said Macleod. 'Or rather, how are you going to? I've got to go shopping for Jane's present this afternoon. Can't hold back that for something as trivial as this.'

Hope smiled. 'First thing we do is we get a list of all the places that have had help from the trust and work done. Then we go through all the history and find out if Blessed Dumpher ever played his flat tune there.'

'That sounds like great fun,' said Macleod.

'Just wait till Perry hears it. And that Ross isn't here to collate a lot of stuff. He's good at that—Ross.'

'Somebody else had better get good at it then,' said Macleod.

He disappeared out of the office, leaving Hope. Within ten minutes, she had the team organised, and they spent the rest of the day on the computer and phoning, asking about Dumpher and his inability to play music.

It was about mid-afternoon when Perry suddenly stormed out again from the office.

'Follow him,' said Hope, looking over at Susan.

'That means I've got to go downstairs on my crutches. He'll be way outside. You know what he does? He goes outside. He stands about three feet from the smoking area and seems to be unable to inhale anything.'

'But you can talk to him. The two of you were getting on

well.'

'Hope, if you don't mind me saying, my leg is sore. No, it's not there. I know you can't see it, but it is sore. Can you speak to him, please?'

Hope nodded, turned and walked down the stairs, wishing she'd brought her jacket as she stepped outside. There was no sun on this summer's day and the wind was cool, probably from the north. As she walked over in her t-shirt and jeans, Perry could see her coming. He quickly put something behind his back.

'You all right?' asked Hope.

'I'm fine,' said Perry.

'Really?' said Hope. 'You see, the thing is, you're either trying to have a cigarette and covering it up, or currently, you're on fire because there's a trail of smoke coming out from behind your head.'

Perry produced his hands from behind his back and puffed on a cigarette.

'I can't,' he said. 'I just—'

'It's all right,' said Hope.

'No, it's not. It's not. It's not all right,' said Perry. 'I've been trying, but it's not getting any better.'

Poor man, thought Hope. *He's really overcome with her.* And he can't talk to her about it because clearly they're not that close yet.

'Perry, why are you giving up cigarettes?'

'They're bad for your lungs. Hadn't you heard?'

'They were bad for your lungs when you joined us and you still smoked, anyway. Why are you giving up cigarettes?'

'I thought it was something she would like,' he blurted.

'Susan?'

'Susan,' said Perry. 'Don't tell anybody else but, well, she's, you see what she's like.'

Hope stood for a moment and almost pitied him.

'Take it she doesn't feel the same way then.'

'No,' said Perry.

'I have to ask this. Is it affecting your work together?'

'It's not.'

'Dumpher's flat tune. I need places and I need them soon,' said Hope. 'If you need to smoke, or if you want to smoke, please do. It's entirely up to you. But if you're going to give up cigarettes, you've got to give them up for you, Perry. You can't do stuff for other people. It doesn't work.'

'So I'm finding out,' he said. He took another drag and then put the cigarette out on the side of the shelter built for smokers, before dropping the cigarette butt into the bin.

'Come on,' said Hope. 'Back at it. Or I'll send you out to help Macleod buy a present for his partner.'

'Threats,' said Perry, almost laughing. 'You don't have to hit me with threats.'

Hope placed a call to Ross to find out he was in the hospital with his young child. It looked like the child had whooping cough. Ross wasn't sure when he'd get back to work. Hope told him not to worry about it and rejoined her team of two detectives, thinking she might have to call some constables to work on this as well.

'I think we've got something,' said Susan. 'I think it might have something to do with, well, there's an ancient stone circle. There's talk there about a flat tune.'

'There's also a possible historic castle,' said Perry. 'Dumpher was once a lord. It's tenuous though; I'm not sure it's the right one.'

'It's okay; it's ideas, and ideas are what we need,' said Hope.

Hope continued to work until at five o'clock, Macleod marched into the office. 'Have you thought about the wind farm?'

'What wind farm?'

'Up Tain way. Dumpher is a small site near it. Electricity pylons and substation.'

'Are you for real?' asked Hope.

'What do you mean?' asked Macleod.

'An electricity substation called Dumpher beside a wind farm. That's not a cryptic clue. That's not even a broadsheet cryptic clue. That is above all, ridiculous.'

'We're not making the rules on this one, Hope,' said Macleod. 'We're just trying to work out what the rules are.'

'Fair enough, Seoras. You joining us?'

'I'm going upstairs to get my secretary to wrap this present up. And then, I'm meant to be going home to take Jane out for dinner. I can give you an hour.'

Macleod sat with the team, wondering if anything that they were bringing forward was actually of any use. He disappeared off later at six. And when they got to ten o'clock that night, Hope called it a day.

'We're all tired and we all need to get rest,' she said. 'Well done, Perry. Not another cigarette today.'

'Very grumpy, though. I'm going to go to bed. Go out first though,' he said, 'and get something proper to eat.'

'What's proper mean?' asked Susan.

'Fried chicken,' said Perry. 'And chips. And a diet coke, just for the irony of it.'

'I'll come with you,' said Susan. Hope looked across at Perry. She found it difficult to read him. Was he happy at this, or was he disappointed because to be in her company and know that she wanted nothing more than to be a colleague could be worse, couldn't it?

'Are you joining us?' asked Perry.

Hope was exhausted. She needed to go home to unwind. She also wondered if, maybe, just maybe, she and John could get half an hour together of, well, close time, not lay-on-the-bed-exhausted time.

'I think I will,' said Hope, thinking that her two colleagues needed somebody with them. 'I'm going to call John, though,' she said. 'He's going to come with us, if that's okay.'

'More the merrier,' said Susan.

'Right then. Make sure we got police patrols around those three sites. I'll get on with it tomorrow.'

'Of course,' said Perry. He turned and got his jacket before bringing Susan's back to her. She stood up on her good leg, put on her coat with Warren's help,

and then hopped her way out to the front door of the station. As she got there, she paused.

'You okay?' asked Hope. There came no reply. Suddenly, Susan collapsed to the ground. Perry came thundering down the stairs behind Hope. But Hope was down first.

'Are you—'

'I don't know what that was,' she said. 'I just felt the wall collapse again. I just collapsed with it. Wasn't unconscious. I was fully aware. I knew there was no wall and yet I just collapsed.'

'Should I get you home?'

'Don't,' said Susan. 'Home is where I think about it all the time.'

'Well then, why don't you come to mine?' said Hope,

realising that she was suddenly going to not get any alone time with John if she did this.

'That's a good idea,' said Perry to Susan.

'But fried chicken first,' said Susan. 'Our Perry here needs it.' Hope smiled at the two of them. After a tough day, although the jokes were weak, at least they were still joking.

Chapter 13

Hope briefly dropped into the office the next morning. They had uniformed officers patrolling at different sites, loosely connected to the letter's clue. However, the team would go out to specific sites once they had narrowed down the options and found credible targets for the bomber. Uniformed officers who passed by the sites through the night had reported no noticeable activity.

Plain clothes officers would today check sites, and then stake them out, once the most likely targets were decided upon. Hope stood in her office, watching the team file in. Ross was the only missing member. His kid was still not clear from the whooping cough that was assailing him, and so Hope told him to remain. Because of this, she'd co-opted Macleod to look after one site.

Susan Cunningham limped into the office beyond Hope's, her crutches swinging, and she had a rather reserved look on her face. Behind her was Perry, carrying a bag, issuing instructions about what to do next. Their conversation was not quiet.

'I'm fine, Perry. Let's just grab the stuff and go. She might not even be in yet.'

'She's been in for a bit,' said Hope, having opened her door.

'Hope,' said Susan. 'We're just getting off now. Sorry, I'm a little bit—'

'She had another episode,' said Warren.

'That's all right. Don't have to panic,' said Hope. 'Are you sure you're okay?'

'No, but you need me at the moment. You need us.'

Susan turned away, making for her desk, opening a couple of drawers, taking out several bits of paper and notebooks, before stuffing them into the bag that Perry was carrying for her. Having done this, she turned and began scooting away, back to the door. Hope intercepted her.

'Give it a thorough check, you two, okay? I know it's a stone circle, but I want you to do a thorough check, Susan. We're looking at an ancient circle, or the flat tune, as it was known in the Gaelic.'

'It'd be a pretty weird place to hide a bomb,' said Susan, 'but we'll cover it. You got the jackets, Perry? It looks like rain.'

'Coming,' he said.

Susan pushed herself off, heading out of the office, and Perry stopped quickly beside Hope. 'She's not right. She shouldn't be doing this.'

'All she's doing is stake out. Told her not to get involved in anything, and besides, she's got you with her.'

'I know,' said Perry, 'I know, but even so.'

'I'm down Ross.'

'How's the little mite?' asked Perry.

'Ross texted me this morning. Not over it yet, still in the hospital.'

'I hope he gets better,' said Perry. He readjusted the bag on his shoulder and hurried out after Susan Cunningham. Hope watched him, thinking he looked more like a husband than a partner. Maybe she should watch that. As she went to turn back to her office, there was a cough from behind her.

'Excuse me; reporting for duty, ma'am.'

Hope turned round. 'You can cut that out,' she said to Seoras, as he stood, grinning at her.

'Just here, on time, ready to go.'

'You've got the wind farm. You okay with it? Understand what you're to do?'

'I'm taking a constable with me. I'll be fine. It's like one of those schemes where they look after the aged.'

'Seoras, shut up!' said Hope. 'Just because you're delighted to be out of the office. Are you missing a meeting today?'

'I'm missing three meetings today. One of them was a budget one,' said Macleod, beaming.

'Seriously though,' said Hope, 'are you okay with this? You need to check the area. But quietly.'

'It's a wind farm. How do you quietly check a wind farm?' mused Macleod.

'Put on a rain jacket, some leggings, walking boots, get a map and pretend you're hiking.'

'That'll work,' said Macleod, 'if I owned any of those.'

'You must own—' and then she caught his face. 'Don't need that today,' she said. 'Go on; we'll be in contact.'

'Yes, boss,' said Macleod. She watched him turn away, almost skipping out of the office. Was stepping up to do most of the paperwork and the main meetings really taking that much out of him? Was it really that much of a bother that he . . .

It didn't matter, did it? Hope needed to get out to her Dumpher. It was a historic castle, albeit a small one, over towards the west coast.

She quietly walked down the stairs, jacket now around her shoulders, thinking about what was ahead. She'd team up with some constables from that side of the mainland. Seven-thirty! She'd better get on the move.

It wasn't good being down Ross, and she didn't enjoy having to bring Macleod in. It felt wrong. Seoras was good. He'd team up with you, and he wouldn't take charge. When he had taken charge, she'd felt it. She'd felt it when they'd stripped her of the job last time, giving it to him because it was a big one, and Clarissa had been in on the side. Yes, it had been a big job. Yes, there were lots of public and press. But, at the end of the day, it was something she could have handled. Maybe he was making a point with his boss talk. She loved him deeply. She really did.

The problem with heading out to the west, though, was it was taking her away from John. Last night, she'd been too tired. And well, things needed to be right. This wasn't a mechanical process she was going through. This was about the start of their life. The start of more. The start of another one coming into it. She got into her car in the car park and Hope sat behind the wheel for a moment. She looked in the rear-view mirror.

She could see a car seat there. One for a toddler in a few years. She'd seen them about. Or would it be the baby in the back gurgling? How would she be as a mum? She thought of Ross and the whooping cough he was dealing with. She shook her head.

Would it be compatible? A child in this work? She started the car.

* * *

Macleod opened the boot of the car and lifted out a set of waterproof trousers. He pulled them on before slipping out of his comfortable shoes and into a pair of boots. He told the constable with him to remove all the police paraphernalia and wrap up in a jacket too. Fortunately, the officer had one in his car when he had met with him. Together they set out towards the turning windmills ahead of him.

'Corn, isn't it?' said Macleod.

'Yes, it is, Detective Chief Inspector.'

'It's an unusual name,' said Macleod. He looked at the lad. He could only have been, what, twenty-one? Fresh. Well-built though, if a little tall. He was looking down at Macleod. Was he taller than Hope? Possibly. Maybe an inch.

'How exactly do we look for bombs, sir?' asked the constable.

'Seoras. My name's Seoras. Seoras Macleod. Okay, we're working together. Call me Seoras. Not inspector, not sir. That's all gone now, so we've got to get on with it.'

'I understand that,' said Corn.

'And on that basis, what's your name?'

'Daniel. Daniel, sir. Oh, sorry. Seoras.'

They walked together in silence for a moment but it was clear the constable wanted to ask something.

'What's Seoras?' he blurted.

'I'm sorry?'

'Seoras? What's Seoras? What is that name? I don't know it,' said Daniel.

'It's Gaelic. It's kind of like, well, the best translation, I guess, would be George.'

'Gaelic? I don't know any Gaelic,' said Daniel.

'It's all right,' said Macleod. 'I speak English.'

'You speak Gaelic as well?'

'I do. A bit. Not very good—at least, that's what they'd tell you. Enough to get by if I went home. Don't use it very often. Home and I, well, let's just say we're uncomfortable company for each other at times.'

'Have you been over here long?' asked Daniel.

'Worked Glasgow for a long time, after I left the island.'

'Which island?' asked Daniel.

'Isle of Lewis. Born and bred there. Married there. Widowed there.'

Macleod walked on and then realised that probably wasn't the kindest thing to offer up to the young lad.

'We're looking for anything unusual,' said Macleod. 'Anything that . . . well . . .'

'What's unusual on the side of a wind farm?'

'Anything really, I guess,' said Macleod. 'Check for power banks though, that look strange. Any boxes attached to it that don't look right.'

Daniel looked out ahead of him. 'See the clouds rolling,' he said, 'a little bit of rain coming in a minute.'

Macleod pulled his hood up on his jacket. *Brilliant*, he thought, *just brilliant*.

* * *

Susan sat in the passenger seat of the car, rubbing her good leg. It was causing her pain. At least she thought it was causing her pain. She'd marched round the ancient stone circle, 'the flat tune' as it had been called. And in truth, it was bugging her, this leg, because she hadn't really worked it that hard.

'Are you all right?' asked Perry.

'Perry, it's every two damn minutes. "Are you all right? Are you okay?" I get you care, but for the love of . . . please, just . . . just treat me like I'm normal.'

She tried to give him a smile, but she clearly had hurt his feelings. 'You got the crisps?' she asked.

'In the bag down by you,' said Perry without looking at her. She reached forward and her leg gave a twinge that caused her to whimper. Perry went to say something and then stopped.

'It's all right; you can ask about that. Clearly, I'm in pain from that.'

'Good leg again?'

'Yeah,' she said.

'May I?' said Perry, reaching forward with his hands.

It was worth a go, she thought. 'Okay,' said Susan. Perry reached down and pulled the trouser leg up and began to rub along Susan's leg. It was soothing, very soothing. He clearly had a knack for what he was doing. Although she wasn't sure if he was reaching the right muscles or not. She leaned back in the car seat. 'That's lovely, Perry,' she said suddenly. 'That's really good.'

He rubbed away at her leg and Susan watched Perry. He turned and smiled at her. 'I'm sorry if I'm being a bit . . . It's just I . . . well . . . well, you know.'

'I know,' says Susan, 'but we're here for a job.'

'There's nothing on the stones. And there's nobody here,' said Perry.

'It is nine in the morning, though,' said Susan. 'Not many people come marching out to a stone circle like this at nine in the morning.'

'Not many people come out here at all. Look at the car park,' said Perry. 'You could fit about four cars in here if you're lucky. There's not even a visitor centre. It's a plaque. Why on earth would you want to blow something like this up?'

'Practice. Nobody else is likely to get hurt. Look at the surrounding terrain, Perry. At least you could watch it.'

Perry let go of her leg, looking to sit back up. 'More, please,' said Susan.

He smiled as he went down and began rubbing her leg again. *I probably shouldn't let him do too much of this,* she thought. *I don't want to give him the wrong impression. But, in fairness, he is damn good at it. And besides, There's nothing else to do here. This is going to be a damp squib.*

* * *

Hope stood outside the historic castle of Dumpher. It was small, barely a castle at all, given the ruin it was in. And not famous. She'd gone over it with a fine-tooth comb and was now sitting in the car alongside a constable from the west coast. They'd been sitting there most of the day. It was five o'clock and nothing had happened.

There'd been three visitors. Two Americans and a woman with her dog in a camper van. Hope rang the rest of the team, but they were saying nothing.

'Looks like a bust, this one,' she said to the constable beside her. Hope felt frustrated. She wanted to get on with this case. There wasn't anything to get on with. That was the problem. Nothing else doing. Solace had got them nowhere. They needed more, needed a breakthrough. Thankfully, no one, other than that first man, was dead. Everyone else got through it unscathed.

But Hope thought about the grand finale. A killing time was coming. And her time was running out.

Chapter 14

Andreas had not been working at the Tourist Information Centre for long, but he enjoyed Aviemore. He'd visited on holidays, routing over from Scandinavia and now, having done a university course and looking for work, he'd found some here in Aviemore. He skied when the snow allowed, walked through the woods, and enjoyed the weather that battered the highlands. Andreas felt he was free out here and at least the Tourist Information Centre kept him up to date with all the different areas and places he could visit.

The Tourist Information Centre was built on a former church. This Andreas knew, because part of the building had a wall in it from that time. However, considering he'd read up on everywhere else, what he hadn't done, was go deeply into the history of that church.

It had been difficult to find, very difficult, but he had in his satchel a book, first written in 1800, although the copy he had was a reprint from the 1950s. It was no longer in circulation, but it was entitled, *Little Known Histories of Little Known Places*. At least that was the modern title. The old one was much longer.

Andreas looked around the Tourist Information Centre and

it was dead. He'd come in for the early shift, half-past eight. The doors had been open for a while, but no one was about. There'd been a festival in the town the previous night. Maybe people were nursing their hangovers or were just simply tired. He pulled the book from his satchel, opened it in front of him at the bookmarked page he'd closed at the previous night.

The book informed him that the church had been built because of a revelation. A monk had decided that he needed to put roots down somewhere to honour God and had built the small chapel that the Tourist Information Centre was now built on.

Andreas thought he heard something, like a ticking sound. *Strange,* he thought. He shook his head then went back down to his book. The monk was little-known and had passed out of history. But, the book said he was instrumental because he was one of the few who followed their vision.

The book really wasn't much cop, was it? And you wondered who it was written by. Maybe it was the transcription. Clearly, the words had been updated for the modern tongue. Maybe it was whoever was bringing it to today's audience that had made a mess of the book.

There was that ticking sound again? Ticking away.

Andreas looked back down at the book. The monk was called Dumpher. Andreas stopped. Dumpher? Unusual name. What is Dumpher?

An alarm rang, like the alarm from an old-style clock beside your bed. The two bells between the hammer clanged either side of the hammer, ringing away. It rang in Andreas's ears for approximately two seconds. Then came the explosion.

Andreas was thrown to one side, but he didn't remember that when they found him. He remembered nothing. He didn't even remember the name of the monk, Dumpher.

* * *

'You were at three different sites,' said Jim, the assistant chief constable. 'How do you do that, Seoras? How do we end up with three different sites and somewhere else gets blown to smithereens?'

'Don't,' said Macleod as they walked along the corridor. Hope was in their wake.

'It wasn't blown to smithereens,' she protested. 'It was a minor explosion. He's going to be all right.'

'Thankfully,' said Jim. 'They're wanting a press conference, I'm sure. You'd better get yourself out there,' said Jim, turning round to Hope. 'How many explosions is that?'

'Six,' said Macleod.

'Six,' said Jim. 'We're darn lucky that nobody's died, except for that first one.'

'No,' said Macleod. 'We're darn unlucky that one person's died. They haven't intended to kill anyone. The first one was an accident.'

'Doesn't matter. If you're ever drunk in a car, you can be lucky enough not to hit someone. This guy's nuts. Clearly.'

'No,' said Macleod. 'He's not nuts. Hope, you best get off. I'll talk to the Assistant Chief Constable and deal with the press conference. Find me something.'

Hope nodded.

'They've been on my phone since this morning,' said Jim. 'Been ringing me since this thing happened, wanting you in front of them.'

'They always want me,' said Macleod. However, Jim was

bothered.

'Do you want to take the case? Do you want to—'

Macleod stopped in the corridor. Jim turned to face him.

'Never ask me that again. I took the last one because they insisted. You undercut her. She knows what she's doing. There's just no evidence. There's just nothing there to go on. And in that regard, I need her. I need her on it. She'll work it through.'

'What's this about Ross? He's not in?'

'His child had whooping cough and was in the hospital. If we need more people, I'll ask for them. I'll pull Clarissa in, Patterson, whoever.'

'They're not going to be happy,' said Jim.

'Jim,' said Macleod. 'They're never happy. They're never happy until it's solved and then the next one happens and they're unhappy again. It's a cycle of unhappiness. It's called management.'

Jim stared at Macleod for a moment and then he burst out laughing. 'You're some operator, Seoras. Just find me something, yes? Find me something. Something I can give them.'

'I've got nothing to give them. Let's get it done,' said Macleod. 'Straighten your tie and jacket.'

'Don't worry about it,' he said to Jim. 'It's not you they're going to be asking the tough questions of.'

* * *

Hope stood amidst the wreckage of the Tourist Information Centre in Aviemore. The glass had been blown out, and she watched from a slight distance as Susan Cunningham hopped here and there in a white coverall suit.

'Hope,' said a voice beside her.

'Perry, how are we doing?'

'Jona's looking into it. Andreas Sorensen was the injured party. They've taken him up to Raigmore. I popped in to see him. I'm just back myself. He doesn't remember much.'

'And he's the normal man for the Tourist Information Centre.'

'Scandinavian chap. Came to university here. Now he's working in the Information Centre. Came in about half eight in the morning. Said he heard an alarm going off, a ticking before that, and then doesn't remember much.'

Hope looked over and saw Jona Nakamura, the Asian forensic lead in Inverness, but also her friend. The Asian woman smiled as she walked over towards Hope.

'Oh, this one's a bit more interesting. He put a clock there.'

'He's activated it with a clock.'

'No. There's the normal detonation device, the normal type of explosive. But there was a clock beside it. Not wired up to anything, but set up.'

'He's got into the tourist information centre and set it up,' said Hope, shaking her head. 'CCTV?'

'Got some. But it doesn't cover the entire store, as far as I'm aware. Shall I just send it to Ross?'

'Ross is out of action.'

'Why?' asked Jona.

'Child gone down with the whooping cough. He's in the hospital. Apparently getting out today, though.'

'Where do I send it?'

'Give it to Perry in the meantime.'

'What else do you think's happening here? asked Hope.

'Same pattern. The bomb blast was far enough away, or should have been far enough away from our young man. However, he sat a little closer than probably would have been expected. No one was in, so by the looks of it, he was at one end of the table, and he had a book open, reading.'

'That's why he's injured then.'

'He was just too close. In the middle of the table, he probably would have had damaged eardrums. That's about it,' said Jona. 'Don't get this. Why blow up here?'

'It's on the list,' said Hope. 'It's on the list of funding applications. Fixed up by a firm called Dramness Builders.'

'But it's not part of the clue, is it?' asked Jona. 'I heard there was a clue,'

'Yes, Dumphers, Dumphers Flat Tune,'

A member of Jona's team came out with a large plastic evidence bag and inside it was a book lying open.

'What's that?' asked Hope.

'It's the book,' said the young man, 'that the victim was reading.'

'What is it?'

'It's about ancient places, as far as I can make out.'

'Let me see a moment,' said Hope. She looked down at the pages, but the book had been folded over slightly. There was a bookmark lying in it, though.

'Can we take that out and have a look at the book, the page that's bookmarked?'

Jona nodded, put on some gloves, and carefully took the book out. She flipped the pages back, and Hope looked down.

'This is about a monk,' she said.

Jona was looking beside her. 'A monk called Dumpher.'

'No,' said Hope. 'How did we miss that? How did we miss

that?' She continued to read. 'This place, this was built on the old church that Dumpher built. Dumpher. He had a habit of praising God, but didn't have a voice to hold a tune.' Hope looked at the ground.

'Did that fit with the clue you got?' asked Jona.

'One hundred percent. How did we miss that?'

'Might not be a common book.'

'Is that the point though? Were we meant to miss it? Were we?'

There was a crash and she turned to see Susan Cunningham collapsed on the ground. She'd been walking along outside the ruined building when a crutch had slipped on a piece of glass, sending Susan to the ground. Perry was there in an instant, helping her up, but Susan clearly had hurt her knee on landing.

She's not going well, thought Hope. *She's not going well at all.* She turned away.

'You all right?' asked Jona.

'No,' said Hope.

'Do you want a couple of minutes?'

'Yes,' said Hope.

The two women marched over to the forensic wagon, and Jona opened up the back of it. There were two people inside it, but she asked for the room. They stepped out of the wagon and Hope climbed in behind Jona. She sat down in one chair and Jona stood, her smaller size, bringing her face to face with Hope.

'What is it?'

'The case. It's not going anywhere. There's nothing to do. There's no—'

'No?' said Jona. 'What is it?'

'The team, they're just, they're everywhere. They're a mess.

Ross is off, we've got Susan falling apart, Perry half absorbed with her. There's just—'

'No,' said Jona, 'what is it?'

Hope suddenly felt tears welling in her eyes. Jona reached out with her hands, and hugged her tight as Hope cried on her shoulder.

'What is it?' said Jona.

'It's silly,' said Hope. 'It's really silly. In the middle of all this, it's really silly.'

'Tell me. It's me,' said Jona. 'You're never silly to me.'

'I just want a baby,' said Hope. 'I just want a baby!'

Jona held her tight as the sudden emotion ran over Hope. This desire, this hunger, this feeling of wanting to be a mother seemed to absorb her. After a few minutes, she broke off. Hope wiped her face down.

'It's ridiculous, isn't it?' she said. 'I've got all this on my plate. I've got somebody bombing places. He's telling me there's going to be a grand finale. He might end up killing people and I just want a baby.'

'No,' said Jona. 'It's lovely. It's absolutely lovely.'

'It'll never work though, will it? Look at me. Look at the way I am. Look at Ross.'

'Ross had a few more insurmountable problems to becoming a father than you do to becoming a mother,' said Jona. 'You've just got to do it.'

'Yes,' said Hope. 'You're right.' She stood up and went to leave, but Jona caught her hand.

'Anytime,' she said.

Hope stepped back out of the wagon and picked up her phone to call Macleod. She wasn't looking forward to explaining to him how they missed it. He'd ask all the questions, he'd go through all the processes, but hey, they just missed it.

Chapter 15

Hope eventually made the office that evening at around about ten. She had told Perry and Susan Cunningham to go home, and to come in early the next morning. There wasn't a lot they had to go on. Investigations had seemed to come up with very little except for an explanation of what the cryptic clue meant.

Jona was still working on the explosives, but tracing them was difficult. They were fairly common, but there was no direct marker to show where they had come from. The detonation devices again, although they'd been worked on and customised, their basic build could have been bought from anywhere.

Hope slogged her way up the steps and into the office. She sat down behind her own desk, pondering on what to do with the investigation. Was she missing something? Did she need to make something else happen with it? There just wasn't anything there.

There was a knock on her door. She looked up and said, 'Come in,' recognising the face on the other side.

'How are you doing?' asked Macleod as he walked in.

'We haven't come up with anything. If that's what you're

wanting, I've got nothing for you to give out. I've got—'

'I didn't ask that,' said Macleod. 'I asked how you were doing.'

'Rubbish,' said Hope. Then she had a sudden thought. *Has Jona been talking to him?*

'No one's been talking to me,' he said.

'What?'

'I said no one's been talking to me.'

She suddenly thought, *What's up? Is he coming in because somebody said I'm not at my best? Has somebody said something else?*

'You should go home. You should go to see that lovely man of yours and you should put this all behind you for a few hours.'

'Sometimes you don't—'

'Whatever you do,' said Macleod, 'I don't need details. Go for a meal, go to the cinema. Do something else.' Macleod looked at her table. 'You realise you haven't got a cup of coffee on that desk?'

He turned and walked out. She saw him in the outer office go across to the coffee machine. Hope shook her head. She watched him do it. That was the thing about Macleod. When he was the boss running it, everybody ran to him. But he could just as easily help others. He wasn't a man who thought of himself above anything.

And yet he was quite staid, even static in his opinions.

Hope could hear someone outside coming up the stairs towards the office. Usually at this time of day, the upper offices weren't open as most people had gone home. Unless you were working late through the night on a case.

Downstairs was always a hive of activity. Uniform, here, there, and everywhere. But upstairs, it should have been settling down. She wondered who was coming in. Within another thirty seconds, she knew. Alan Ross stepped into the office, dressed in a suit with a shirt and tie underneath.

'Let me do that,' said Ross, seeing Macleod making the coffee.

'No, you don't,' said Macleod. 'Your boss is in there; go and see her.' Ross went to turn, but Macleod stopped him. 'How's the wee one?' he said.

'Out of danger. He's okay. Take a few days. It'll be a week.'

'Are you okay to be here?' asked Macleod.

There was a curt nod from Ross, and he marched off into Hope's office.

'And what are you doing here?' asked Hope.

'He's going to be okay. I'm back. I did some work at home. Thought you should know what I've got.'

'Seoras, would you hurry with that coffee?' shouted Hope out of the door.

'Just because I'm making the coffee doesn't give you the right to talk to me like I'm an office boy,' said Macleod. 'Your inspector—your boss—will bring the coffee in a minute when he's ready.'

'Alan's got something,' said Hope.

The one thing you couldn't do with Macleod was get him to hurry coffee. And Hope was on tenterhooks. Ross had come in, left his child, albeit on the mend, to come in at ten o'clock at night to pass on information. More than that, he was dressed in a suit, shirt, and tie. He was staying. He wasn't going home anytime soon. So, this must be important.

Macleod eventually wandered in with the coffees, putting the tray down on Hope's table and then handing them out.

'Well, now that the coffee boy is finished,' said Hope, giving a wry smile to Macleod, 'maybe we can get on with the investigation.'

'What have you got, Ross?' asked Macleod.

'Okay, boss, all the targeted locations were getting funding. Yes?'

'Well, we knew that,' said Hope. 'And lots of other places that didn't get funding weren't targeted.'

'But they weren't just getting funding. If you look at who did the work, it's subcontracted out, which is where the difficulty comes. And it's only when that tourist information centre got bombed, that I realised I could speak to someone on the board who looked into it for me. All these buildings, they've all been worked on by Dramness Builders Limited.'

'Dramness Builders Limited,' said Hope. 'You sure?'

'Of course, I'm sure. That's why your ancient stone circle wasn't blown up. Your controversial new wind farm wasn't touched. Not Dramness Builders. The historic Castle. Not Dramness Builders. Tourist Information Centre. Built on a broken-down church, but restored and built up by Dramness Builders. Local church in Ullapool. All Dramness Builders.

'Dramness Builders get given a lot of this work, including that lighthouse in Skye. It's subcontracted work, which is why we didn't pick it up, but they're heavily involved. The pharmacy in Inverness, Dramness Builders did work on that; they worked on the primary school in Stornoway too, sent people over.'

'The frozen food processing factory?' said Macleod. 'What would they have to do with that?'

'The main office,' said Ross. 'Main office was part funded, built by Dramness Builders.'

'But why target them, Alan?' asked Hope.

'I don't know,' said Ross. 'All I know at the moment is that there's something going on. They're heavily involved. They've been doing repairs in all these situations or building from scratch and these sites have been targeted. I don't think the funding is the issue. I think Dramness Builders are the issue.'

'What do you know about them, then?'

'I don't. Let's find out.'

'How are we going to do it?' asked Hope.

'Well, I get online—work out what I can. Their offices, they've got quite a few different ones. We could speak to them.'

'Can we do that? Get hold of them now,' asked Hope.

'Hope,' said Macleod. 'Calm down. They're builders. They won't be there.'

'But this is a murder investigation,' she said. 'This is—'

'And your clamour and zeal are exemplary,' said Macleod. 'However, I know you want to go after this, hook, line, and sinker. But go in prepped. See what we can find out through the night. Then go at them first thing in the morning. You don't know where this is coming from.

'What is it? Is it somebody who's had work done by them? Is it a disgruntled employee? Is it somebody within the board? Is there something going on there? A rift between the owners? Is it a rival company who is out to get them? We just don't know yet.'

Hope picked up the phone. 'Oh, Perry and Cunningham can get their backsides in here. Sort this out.'

'I can do it,' said Ross. 'It's what I'm good at.'

'No, I want everything. We'll bring them in.'

Macleod sipped on his coffee, looking at Hope.

'Are you stopping?' she asked.

'Do you need me?'

'Somebody's got to make the coffee,' said Hope.

Macleod gave her a scowl and then laughed. 'You're going to need fed as well. We don't want to leave it too long. Unless you want the canteen food, I can pop out and get something.'

'Chinese,' said Ross, instantly. 'I'm famished.'

'I'm on it,' said Macleod. 'I'll see you shortly.'

By the time Macleod had returned with the food, Susan Cunningham and Perry were sitting at their desks. Ross was engrossed in his screens. Macleod took the food downstairs, making the canteen night shift keep it in the warm oven. The canteen wasn't as well stocked through the night. Most of the meals were for the microwave. There was a small staff on, but it wasn't unknown for food to be brought in from outside.

At four in the morning, Ross finally looked up from his screens.

'You got somewhere?' asked Hope, coming out of her office.

'I have indeed.'

'Good,' said Macleod. 'I'll go get us some food, set up a few tables, we'll sit round it and chat for a bit. Talk about what's happening.' Then he looked over at Hope. 'If that's okay with you?'

Hope nearly burst out laughing. 'Okay, food boy, go get the grub.'

'You keep this up, I'm really not going to be happy,' said Macleod.

'Is the coffee filled up now?' asked Hope. Macleod nodded, laughing.

Five minutes later, the team were sitting down, scoffing their fried rice and several other delicacies. The morning light was pervading from outside.

'What have you got, Ross?' asked Hope.

'From off the web, forums and stuff, a lot of employee forums.

They're not a great company to work for. We've also got a trail of complaints from people who they've done jobs for. Shoddy workmanship, alleged corruption. Here's one. "The wall stood up for all of two days before we realised that the cement between the bricks hadn't set properly. Luckily, we managed to prop the wall up before it fell down. Being a primary school, this wasn't a—"'

'Point taken,' said Hope.

'What else have we got?'

'Got a line of former employees lining up talking about them. Cross-referenced through the internet. Different chat sites. And we have lots and lots of broken promises. Promotions, oh, that doesn't happen. Longer working hours for increased pay further down the road.'

'Really,' said Hope. 'They really that bad.'

'Okay, but what about the company itself?' asked Macleod. 'Anything about those who are running it?'

'Dodgy,' said Perry. 'Very dodgy. There's a couple working for them who've been bankrupt before. Seems that their wives are on the board.'

'What else have we got?' asked Hope.

'Well, let's see. It seems to me,' said Susan, 'that they're not looking after disabled people.'

'Oh?' said Macleod. 'What makes you say that?'

'Well, they've got a lot of complaints about equipment put in. You've had people who have worked for them for quite a time, needing work adjustments and complaining they're never done. These people don't look good, not in the slightest.'

'That's fine,' said Hope. 'The issue I've got now is what does all that actually mean? What does that mean to us? Are they being attacked by someone else? Is it an employee? Is it a punter who's not happy? Is it somebody within the company higher up wanting to get rid?'

'But places, worksites, have changed hands several times,' said Ross. 'I've gone back into a lot of their owned buildings, their workstations, where they keep the equipment. They've gone through a number of companies of which some of these guys used to be directors of. These guys look shoddy; they look a shambles.'

'Right,' said Hope. 'So, what do we do? We've got resentment coming up. We've had places highlighted by the bombings, but apart from that one which we think is a mistaken death at the start, nobody's been injured.'

'But he talks about a grand finale' said Perry. 'That's scary. That sounds like they could go for the entire company.'

'Easy,' said Macleod, 'you don't know that. We still don't know who's targeting and from what point of view. Punter, inside worker, disgruntled management. Who knows?'

Hope picked up a spring roll, popped it in her mouth and chewed thoughtfully on it.

'We've got somewhere to start,' she said. 'You've got addresses of management?' she asked Ross.

'Yes,' said Ross. 'List of addresses, everything.'

'In that case, we need to get out there, tomorrow.'

'Tomorrow,' said Ross. 'It's after four.'

'We eat this and get home. Back in for eight. In fact, no, I'll come back in for eight,' she said. 'I'll interview the company owner. Rest of you in here for ten. I might have something by then. I'm going to catch them unawares, though.'

'I'll come with you,' said Ross. 'I'm your sergeant after all.'

'No,' said Hope. 'You've been up with your kid. Get home. If you don't want to go home, see him. And then get back in here.

It's more important than you being with me. Susan needs a rest because of her leg. Perry can look after her.'

'You're not going on your own, are you?' said Ross.

'I'm a big girl, but no. Seoras will come with me.'

'I've got a meeting in the morning,' said Macleod. And then smiled. 'That's another one ticked off.'

Hope shook her head. 'You're meant to set these guys an example.'

'I've been here all night,' said Macleod. 'I've made you the best coffee you've had in about a week. What more example could you want?'

Hope told the team she'd clear the dishes up and sent them home, but Macleod watched as they filed out. Perry was looking after Susan Cunningham all the way down the stairs, and Ross seemed glad to get back to his little fella.

'You get some shuteye, too, Seoras,' said Hope. 'I'll get these.'

'No,' said Macleod. 'You go.'

She turned for a moment. 'My team is my responsibility.'

'Hope, would you go get that coat, and would you get home?'

'I don't need any sleep,' she said. 'I'm buzzing now. I'm absolutely buzzing. We've got somewhere to go. You know what that's like, don't you? You just don't want to go to bed.'

'I know what it's like, and I'll be going home. But you go and see John.'

Hope looked at him, realising he knew so much more than he was saying. Macleod was polite. He wouldn't talk about things that really shouldn't be talked about, if he could get away with it. She turned and grabbed her jacket off the coat rack back in her office. As she walked out, she looked at Macleod, pulling the plates together.

'Thanks, Seoras.'

'Anytime,' he said.

'I'll do the same for you sometime,' said Hope. 'For you and Jane.'

'Me and Jane would have missed the cinema by now,' said Macleod. 'You have to start earlier with us. We don't burn the candle.'

'Who are you kidding?' said Hope cheekily, as she almost tore the door off its hinges

Macleod collected the last of the plates. He smiled to himself. *The team looked better,* he thought. *And he wasn't going to have to go to a meeting tomorrow.*

Chapter 16

Macleod said he would pick up Hope to give her the maximum time at home with John. As he pulled up in front of their flat, he thought the day was going to be a good one. She had said she'd be there at half past seven, and then he'd drive to the offices of Dramness Builders by eight o'clock. He thought about going to the door, but Macleod had been young once. More recently, he'd been old trying to be young with Jane, and so he didn't want to disturb Hope. Macleod saw Hope's partner, John, emerging in jeans and a t-shirt and coming over to the car.

'She says you have to come in. She's in the shower.'

'I don't want to bother you,' said Macleod. 'It's all right. She's entitled to have a shower. I'll be okay here,' said Macleod.

'How's she been,' asked John. He opened the passenger door and climbed in, and Macleod rolled up the window that he'd brought down to allow John to speak.

'It's been tough on her—this case,' said Macleod. 'It's just one of those where you don't get any breaks. You get nothing to start, but we've got something now,' said Macleod.

'You think it'll work out? Or do you think it might be a dead end?' said John.

'No, we're on the right track,' said Macleod. 'How are you, anyway?'

'I'm good,' he said. 'But she's worried.'

'I know,' said Macleod.

'She's worried about the job. She's worried about, well, maybe she hasn't told you. Maybe I shouldn't tell you.'

'You're trying for a kid and you're worried,' said Macleod, 'that it's not going to work. She's worried that the kid's not going to fit in properly. She's seeing Ross and Ross is struggling.'

'I think so. I think that's what it is. But she'll make it work. She's more than capable. She's—'

'She's Hope McGrath, the tall, red-headed detective inspector. She is more than capable. So are you, John. I'm not going to give you any tips, because I can't. I don't have any kids. But you have to be able to give them time. You have to step away from this job. I'm not good at that. Maybe she'll be better. You'll have to help her with that and you'll have to make sure she sticks to it.'

John sat and nodded and then looked over as Hope came running out the front door. She was in jeans and a black t-shirt, and had her jacket on her arm. Her hair was still wet and long, swinging around her face as she ran.

'I like her like that,' said John. 'When she puts the hair up, she becomes Detective Hope.'

'She does,' said Macleod. 'And I apologise for taking a bit of her away from you.'

'You don't take her. She goes voluntarily. It's what she is. She's like you in that, isn't she? Hope's a detective. She's a different sort of one, but she's a detective.'

'Well, she's taller and she's got red hair,' said Macleod. 'And the accent's different.'

John looked at him and gave a laugh. 'Keep an eye on her.'

'I keep an eye on them all,' said Macleod. 'That's my job.'

Hope opened the passenger door. 'Get out, you,' she said.

John stepped out, and she kissed him, brazenly, before climbing into the car. 'You'll be back tonight?' he asked.

'Who knows? See where this goes today.'

'I'm only a call away,' he said. 'Love you.'

'Love you too,' said Hope. She sat back in the passenger seat as Macleod turned on the engine and drove off into the early morning Inverness traffic.

'What are you smiling at?' she said.

'You. Did you good getting a couple of hours with him, didn't it?'

'Oh yes,' said Hope. 'Oh yes!' She reached up behind her head, pulled her hair together, and then slipped over a black tie, pulling her hair into a ponytail. 'Well, it's business time, Seoras, time to get to work.'

Macleod smiled as he drove through the traffic for another fifteen minutes before arriving at the main builder's yard for Dramness Builders Ltd. The forecourt was busy, vans disappearing out to jobs. Macleod and Hope made their way to the building that housed the offices. The front door was locked but inside, a rather perturbed-looking secretary looked up at Macleod and Hope.

'Who are you?' she mouthed through the window.

Hope pulled out her warrant card. 'Detective Inspector Hope McGrath,' she said loudly. 'This is Detective Chief Inspector Seoras Macleod. We want to talk to the owners of Dramness Builders.'

'Do you have an appointment?' said the young woman,

opening the door.

'Do you get who we are? We don't need an appointment. We're here to talk to the owners. If the owners aren't willing to talk, we can have them come down to the station for a chat.'

'Okay. Calm yourselves,' said the woman, rather abruptly.

Macleod looked a little confused and Hope just shrugged her shoulders. The woman made a phone call upstairs and then told them to head straight up. Macleod let Hope lead, and she arrived on a landing with several doors. One said, 'Director Fern Lemon.'

Hope knocked on the door. When there was an answer, it was a gruff man's voice. She opened the door and strode in.

'Director Fern Lemon not in then,' said Hope.

'Fern's my wife. She's a director but I run the company . . . well, along with my brother and my stepbrother.'

'Very good, and you would be?'

'Ian Lemon. My brother is Clive and my stepbrother is Max.'

'Very good, I'm Detective Inspector Hope McGrath, and this is Detective Chief Inspector Seoras Macleod.'

'Oh, I know you,' said Ian. 'Why on earth have I got you here? You're on the murder team, aren't you?'

'I actually cover several areas,' said Macleod, 'but Hope's on the murder team. But we are here in terms of the murder team. We're investigating a death at a frozen food factory in the Highlands. A refrigeration plant blowing up,' said Macleod.

'What's that got to do with me?' asked Ian Lemon.

'Well, you built it, or at least you built the offices beside it. There's also been several other explosions, and each one is at a place that you had a hand in building, or repairing, or adding to. So, you are a direct line of enquiry.'

Ian Lemon narrowed his eyes. 'But what's it got to do with

us?'

'Have you,' asked Hope, 'had any troubles with your employees?'

'None. We're an accredited company. We run well. A lot of the lads have been with us for a long time. What's that got to do with it?'

'The lads have been with you for a long time. You won't have much staff turnover then. How many do you turn over a year?'

'Twenty,' said Ian Lemon.

'Twenty per cent?' said Macleod. 'That's quite high, isn't it?'

'I think that's what we're estimating.'

'That's very interesting,' said Hope. 'On the web, someone who used to work for you said that you're almost at fifty per cent turnover.'

'That's just ridiculous. We wouldn't have any employees left to find. There's only so many skilled tradesmen in the Highlands.'

'What's the accurate figure then?' asked Macleod.

'Thirty-five,' said Ian.

'So you know that you've got trouble with your employees. We've also got a host of complaints.'

'Our work's good.'

'No, it's not' said Macleod. 'Or at least it's not to the liking of your customers or indeed your workers. Yet you seem to be getting lots and lots of jobs where the fund for the Highlands is being used. You've got connections in there.' Macleod stared at him.

'We're going to have to look into this closely,' said Hope. She knew that the man was looking nervous. His hands rubbed together.

'You're looking at the victim here,' said Ian.

Hope looked around her. 'Your offices seem fairly intact.'

'We've been receiving threatening emails for months.'

'Threatening emails?'

'Very much so.'

'Have you reported any of these?' asked Macleod.

'No, we didn't think it'd be—'

'Let me see them,' said Hope. 'I take it they're on your computer.'

'Yeah,' he said.

Hope and Macleod moved to stand behind Ian Lemon as he showed them emails on his computer.

'We're going to have to let our sergeant come in and take a look at where they've come from. Do not touch them. Do not touch your systems until he gets here and says you can.'

'We need our systems. We need to—'

'Not until you're told,' said Hope. 'What else have we got?'

'Look at them,' said Macleod. 'Look at the emails. That letter they wrote to me, it was quite cryptic, wasn't it? The style's very similar in these emails.'

Hope nodded. 'It looks like it. Tell me something. When did you realise that the bombs were going off at the places you had worked?'

'Well, at first, it was just the place we worked at. I think it was after the third or fourth one we started getting these emails and, well, there you go.'

'You didn't think to report them then,' said Macleod. 'I mean, the explosions have been on the news. I know, I've been at the press conferences where the papers and the TV have been clamouring for more detail to fill up airtime and paper with the stories.'

'Well,' said Ian, 'you kind of hope, don't you, that it'll go away.'

'I think you're more worried about your own company. I think you're worried about people looking into it. What's going on? How are you getting these jobs? Is it all legitimate?' asked Hope.

'It's as above board as anyone else,' said Ian Lemon.

Well, that's slightly damning, Hope thought to herself. 'What do you mean by that?'

'There's always a bit of coercion. There's always a bit of greasing the wheels, isn't there?' said Ian.

'Right,' said Hope. 'I'm bringing my full team in. We're going to be looking at your emails; we're going to be looking at your practices; we're going to be looking at everything to do with you and what you've been doing. I have to warn you we've received threatening communications about a grand finale from this bomber. On the face of it, there's a strong possibility it could be about you and your company. I advise you to cooperate with us at every opportunity and to look after yourselves and your employees.'

'You can't just drop that one on me. I've got a business to run; we've got things to do. You can't start—'

'Oh, she can,' said Macleod. 'And I'll back her to the hilt. I'm afraid your chickens are coming home to roost, Mr Lemon. Unfortunately, some of them look like they could cause a pretty big bang.'

'You have to find him, wherever this is. Find this nut job. It is a nut job, isn't it?' rambled Ian.

'Until we get to know who they are and their exact reasons,' said Hope, 'they may be one of the most rational people going.'

'But they've killed someone.'

'They've killed someone accidentally,' said Hope. 'That's our belief. But if they come for you, I think it'll be intentional. So,

I'm going to need to sit and run through what security you've got on sites. I'm going to need to talk about what jobs you've got in the pipeline, where else you're working. Your day just became a long one and involves me,' said Hope.

'I'm just going to step outside,' said Macleod, 'and talk with my colleague and then she'll be back in. I suggest you prepare yourself to be as forthcoming and helpful as possible.'

Macleod nodded to Hope. The pair of them went down the steps and back outside the main building. Once outside, Macleod turned to Hope.

'He's guilty of something,' said Macleod. 'He's panicking. He doesn't want his company looked at. Who knows what we're going to pull out once we go through it?'

'Gives a darn good motive though, for whoever.'

'And whoever is the key thing. We're going to need to find whoever. Emails. Get Ross in immediately. Get him on those. See if we can find out where they're being sent from.'

'I'll also get heavily into looking at the company. Maybe there are some disagreements, bigger than others. Big workforce, though, by the looks of it.'

'Very much,' said Macleod. 'But we can handle it. You can handle it. I'm going to get back to the station. And I'm going to call a meeting with Jim and tell him we're on it. And tell him where we've got to.'

'Don't worry. I'll get you more.'

Macleod nodded. 'I'll send Ross down with the car. Do you want yours brought down?'

'No, the team can sort me. We need to be into this quick though. Grand finale. Can't be that far away.'

'Understand one thing, Hope,' said Macleod. 'We've had these explosions. He's given us a clue to where they're going to be. But in no instance has the bomber told us why? The bomber has never highlighted to us, or the public, what the thing is that's bothering them. Clearly it might be the shoddy workmanship that's going on with this company. It may be more than that. But at some point that's going to be brought out.

'You can't just bomb somewhere after all of this and then justify it afterwards. It'll be brought out before, in some shape or form; there'll be a highlight. There'll be a finger pointing to say, look this is it, this is what it's all about, because at the moment we just have randomly blown-apart buildings.'

'Best get cracking then, hadn't we?'

She watched Seoras get into his car and turn to drive back to the station. Hope turned round. She stopped for a moment, thinking back to the earlier part of the morning. She grinned to herself. *Life's suddenly looking good again; how did that happen? Was she really that fickle? No,* she thought, nor indeed was John. Their relationship was simply that good.

Chapter 17

Hope McGrath sat in the offices of Dramness Builders with her leather jacket hanging on the back of a chair. She felt the sweat run down her face because the room seemed to have no air. It was the conference room, and she spent most of it, that morning and afternoon, speaking to Ian Lemon. Clive Lemon had been in as well. Also Max, the stepbrother. Along with Perry. She'd grilled them.

She'd sent Susan Cunningham out, running round their sites, building up a list of where they were operating. Ross had come in and was working on the emails that had threatened the company. So far, the team had done well. There was also a myriad of employees they'd spoken to. Most of them were very reticent to speak, but a few had commented on just how bad the company was and how they'd been mistreated.

Susan Cunningham had also got into a lot of their records and the employee turnover within the company was indeed palpable. She was trying to pull every name she could from the last couple of years to see if there was anyone there that stood out. However, it would take a long time to check it all through.

Hope was now in the conference room alone, looking round

it. The sweat trickled down her back and also into her front. It made her think about earlier on that morning.

It was funny. She always tried to be professional. But now there was a palpable excitement within her. Not the teenage one of the first time with a lover or of being young and alone. There was a feeling within her she was about to set out on something very different. An unknown part of her life was about to happen. She and John may become three, not two.

There was a knocking at the door and Hope asked them to come in.

'Perry,' she said. She only thought she was sweating until she saw Perry arrive.

'Right,' he said, 'I've told them they can clear off for the day. There's no more we're going to get out of them. Susan's grabbed most stuff. We're just waiting to see if Ross has come up with anything. I've got a ton of records to get through. Susan and I are going to go back to the station to start looking at them.'

'Good,' said Hope. 'I'll follow you up there shortly once I make sure Ross has got everything.'

Perry disappeared, and Hope stood up, grabbing her leather jacket. She flung it over her shoulder rather than wear it due to how warm she felt. Hope trundled along two doors on the landing, to find Ross inside another office. Beside him was a secretary, but she looked rather absent now, staring out of a window.

'How are we getting on, Alan?' asked Hope.

'I think I've got something.'

'Could you excuse us a moment?' he said to the secretary. She was only a young girl, maybe seventeen, maybe nineteen, maybe twenty-two. Hope was having trouble judging them these days. It was a thing that Macleod complained about all the time. He had no idea what age people were, especially at the younger end of the spectrum.

'What's up?'

'Threatening emails have all come from a public library computer in Fort William.'

'Fort William?'

'Yes, I'm just trying to get a hold of them. I think we might keep them open. Let's get over and see if they've got any CCTV, anything like that.'

'You sure? Why don't you pop back and see your lad?'

'I can do this,' said Ross.

'I know you can do it, Alan, but I want you firing on all cylinders. Pop back, phone Angus, tell him you'll meet him at the hospital. Go see your boy, grab a bite to eat. I'll meet you in an hour and a half. Then we'll head down to Fort William.'

'Okay,' said Ross. 'I'll organise meeting someone there.'

'Good,' said Hope.

An hour and a half then to do something. She picked up her phone. She called John and half an hour later was sitting with him in Kessock, just beyond the bridge of the same name at the edge of Inverness. It was a place to watch dolphins apparently, but she hadn't seen any recently. Hope sat with her take-away food, John beside her.

'Where are you going?' he asked.

'I'm heading over to Fort William.'

'You'll be away tonight.'

'Tonight, who knows, maybe longer. We're heading somewhere now with the case. I'm going to see you less until we get it cracked.

'Once it's cracked though,' said John, 'maybe we should make a weekend. Maybe we should—'

'Whatever you want,' said Hope. 'Somewhere, just you and me.'

'Are you still worried?' he said.

'About?'

'Bringing a kid into this. Into your work situation. Into—'

'Completely,' she said. 'But, it's what you and I need. We want to build a family. If that means I have to give up being a detective then so be it. If it means I have to do something different, I will. Maybe even join Clarissa, God forbid, in her treasure hunt. Then, so be it.'

'What is it with Clarissa? Every time you talk about her, it's never complimentary. You tell me how wonderful Macleod is, but Clarissa . . .'

Hope laughed. 'Clarissa was always my opposite number. She was the sergeant who wasn't. She's not me. Clarissa does stuff I wouldn't do, but she gets results I can't.'

'But you get results she doesn't. Don't you?'

'Yeah,' said Hope. 'That's true. It doesn't stop me wanting to be a bit like her at times though.'

'In what way?' asked John.

'She's direct. And she can take you on in a fight.'

'What?' said John. 'She's an older woman. She's like what? Sixties?'

'She's the dirtiest fighter I've ever seen. You don't get a chance. She goes at them before they even know they're in a fight with her,' laughed Hope.

'And you want to be like that? You can fight. You can handle the best of them.'

'Kirsten could handle the best of them. I do all right,' said Hope.

John pulled her close. 'You just be you,' he said. 'I can't think of anyone else I'd like my kid to look at.'

'You're getting soppy in your old age. Do you know that?'

'Yep,' he said, 'completely.'

She left him there about twenty minutes later and picked Ross up from the hospital. They drove down to Fort William, a reasonable drive in its own right, and she let Ross sleep. The man had been at it all through the previous nights. But unlike her, he hadn't slept. He'd gone to see his kid and as he'd put it, just stayed awake. But come to think of it, she hadn't slept either.

Hope grinned to herself as she drove along. She remembered her younger days. She slept little then. But she was still Hope underneath it all. Even as a mum-to-be. She wasn't there yet, but she'd get there.

They arrived at the public library in Fort William at approximately ten o'clock. A rather disgruntled librarian greeted them, with a firm handshake. There was also a comment about how she was missing the latest episode in her drama series. Ross apologised and Hope let him walk through the library with the librarian.

The woman had a large skirt and a cardigan on, despite the obvious warmth of the evening. She seemed to bustle here and there, while Ross glided elegantly.

'CCTV images, we've got up to a month going back,' said the woman. 'I can show you those. I'll take you through it.'

'Show me your system, then leave me to it, please,' said Ross. 'Detective Inspector Hope McGrath will ask you some other questions. Initially, we'll need you to hang about while we look through the CCTV.'

'How long are you going to be?' asked the woman.

'As long as it takes.'

'Well, that's no good, is it?' she said. 'This better be on catch-up.'

Hope raised her eyebrows at Ross.

The pair of them were soon sitting at the library CCTV system. Ross had arranged the dates and quickly arrived at the days and times the public computer was accessed. Hope scanned the screen with him but it was Ross, as ever, who pointed out a suspect.

'That person,' he said, after a couple of hours of looking at the film. 'Each of the days, that person's been in.'

'It's a bit of a grainy image, though, isn't it?' said Hope.

'It is, but he's what? What age would you put him? Sixty?'

'Fifty?' said Hope.

'Somewhere in his fifties or sixties, then,' said Ross. 'But he's got a limp.'

Ross replayed the footage, and it was clear. On each of the occasions, the man had a limp. Hope went back into the library to find the librarian sitting with a cup of tea, and a book in her hand. At no point had she offered tea to them.

'I'd like you to come in and have a look at the video footage with us. See if it's someone you know.'

'I'll just finish this chapter,' said the woman. Hope wanted to tell her to hurry, but it was now midnight and the woman was helping. So, Hope waited two minutes until the woman put her book down and then followed her through.

'Oh, him!' she said. 'He's in all the time.'

'Do you have a name?' asked Hope.

'No,' she said. 'He's in all the time, but he never takes a book out. I've seen him read books, but never take a book out.'

'He's got a limp though, hasn't he?' said Hope.

'A distinctive limp,' she said. 'He's got a whitish beard. His hair's quite slick usually, swept back. I would say he's more into his sixties. Maybe about five feet seven to five feet eleven. Somewhere in there.'

Well, that was fairly wide-ranging, thought Hope. She took more details down, as best she could from the woman, before Ross lifted the video footage he required. He told her that the system would be confiscated and they'd need to use it, but they'd come back in the morning to do that. Hope contacted the local station to see if any of the local officers knew who it was. She coordinated getting a canvas to be done around the area the next day.

'Back up the road or stay here,' said Hope.

'Stay here,' said Ross.

'You sure you don't want to see your kid?'

'No,' said Ross. 'I've been. He's all right. He's getting on. We need to do this. We can pull down Susan and Perry in the morning. Give them a hand if they need it.'

'Will do,' said Hope. They found a hotel with two rooms. Hope made her way to her bed at about one in the morning.

She sat up in it, picked up her phone and called John. An hour later, he told her to get to sleep. But when she'd finished the call, she couldn't. The excitement was back. She reckoned it was the ability now to have something else to focus on and not just this case. It wasn't the fact they were moving forward.

She lay in the bed. If she had to give up this job, would it be that bad? Would she be letting down Seoras? He'd moved to let her in. He'd done so much for her. It was her decision, hers to make. Hope's and John's. That's what he would say.

He'd tell her to do what she wanted to do. That the force would still continue. Even if he wasn't there. She had to remember that. She lay back and looked at the ceiling. Times were changing. Let them change.

Chapter 18

Kelly Tulloch at fifty-seven counted herself lucky to be able to wake up every morning and talk to her listeners. Kelly Tull, as she was known, was an institution in the world of local radio broadcasting. She'd somehow moved from her early days of a teenage and young adult audience into a family vibe.

Even now, when she was realistically becoming a grandma compared to those younger listeners, she still seemed to connect. She brought the family together like some sort of mad auntie.

Dexter was the reason she'd be able to do it, though. And her studio manager was across from her, through the window, with a smile on his face. They were only six minutes out from finishing the show. She broadcasted for two and a half hours every morning and, in truth, the hours were starting to catch her up. But she wouldn't give it up for the world.

Kelly could see into the other studio, where the younger Martin McGregor was soon to take over from her. He'd given her the thumbs up, but that was about as much as she would get out of Martin. Sometimes when they had their own shows, the DJs would talk for a bit, have a bit of banter. Martin wasn't like that. He was calm, professional, and if you met him, he was polite. But he wasn't friendly, not at all buddy-buddy.

Kelly had learned enough from this broadcasting life that she didn't push people to be something they weren't. He did a good show; that's what he was paid to do. Let Martin be Martin. As long as they let her be her. Well, that was fine because they had. She wore bright pink glasses which took over her face. Her eyes were lost somewhere deep in them, far removed from her full, red lips and peroxide-blonde hair.

Kelly made an impact wherever she went. She was never a woman blessed with a stunning figure, but she had a mouth that could speak for the world. Quick-witted and engaging, she'd tried TV once, but it wasn't the same. On TV, you came out looking fat, whatever that camera did to you.

Not being blessed with an incredibly slim figure to start off with, she couldn't stand to see herself on the screen. It was funny. She'd noticed one of those weather girls once. The woman had been up for an eclipse or something, and my goodness, she was sensational. A figure to die for. If anything, maybe even a touch thin, but when Kelly saw the woman on the television screen that night, what that camera did to her was unholy.

She looked like some buxom maiden from the middle ages, weight appearing where weight wasn't. Kelly would never have that.

She put on the final record. She laughed at herself. Record? Those were the days. Nowadays, press a button, line it all up on the screen. She sat back, satisfied, knowing there were just a few words more after the song played out to say, and another show was in the bag.

Kelly still had the headphones on, but something somewhere

was ticking. She removed the right headphone, and the sound grew louder. She took the headphones off completely, placing them on the desk in front of her, and began looking around. Through the glass, her studio manager was looking at her, giving a perplexed look. Kelly put her hand up, clicking her fingers, trying to show that there was a ticking sound.

What is it? Kelly wondered. She stood up from her chair and bent down, looking around the studio, under the desks, and beside the chair. The sound was coming from one cupboard in the corner, wasn't it?

She delicately opened the cupboard. Inside were various old brochures and forms, put away when nobody knew if they should throw them out. But there was also an alarm clock. The second hand was ticking round.

How on earth did an alarm clock get in there? Kelly left the cupboard door open, walked over to the glass and banged on it, shouting at her studio manager, and pointing to the cupboard.

Dexter took one look and started yelling at her. She tried to make out what he was saying, but the man was apoplectic. He was losing it.

Was that 'get out'?

She turned back, to hear the bells clanging. The clock was sounding its alarm. Kelly grabbed the door, opening it by the handle. The next thing she knew, she was thrown across, out into the corridor, her shoulder slamming up against a wall. After that, there was nothing.

* * *

Hope McGrath sighed. There'd been an explosion at the radio

station.

She had raced back as fast as she could from Fort William. Macleod was already on site, saying he'd cover it until she got there. She'd left Ross down in Fort William, looking for him to pick up whatever pieces were there. Perry was sent to accompany Ross, while Susan Cunningham would join Hope at the radio station.

As Hope got there, she saw the barrage of cameras and reporters. She drove up slowly to the line of them, seeing them all squirm up against the windows of her car. Her uniformed colleagues moved them aside and let Hope into the car park of the radio station.

She stepped out once she'd parked and saw Macleod waving at her from near the main building. Hope walked over to see a grimace on his face.

'What happened?' she asked.

'Another bomb. Another one we don't think was meant to harm anyone.'

'Why do you say that?'

'Studio One was doing the morning breakfast show,' said Macleod.

'Kelly Tulloch?' said Hope.

'Same one. She's in Raigmore. Broken shoulder. She got lucky.'

'How so?'

'She was in the studio finishing off the show for the morning and Miss Tulloch heard a ticking and opened the cupboard.'

'And what happened?' asked Hope.

'There was an explosion. But she had gone to tell the studio manager at the window that there was a problem. He had told her to get out. She was just getting through the door when the explosion happened. It blew her right out into the hall.'

'So why do you say she was lucky? Why do you think they weren't there to harm her?'

'Simply, the bomb wasn't meant to go off at that point,' said Macleod. 'It was intended that it go off in the middle of the night when Studio One isn't being used. One of the cleaners saw the clock, picked it up, turned the clock dial.'

'But wouldn't that have set it off earlier?'

'Apparently not. Jona now reckons that they're actually wired up, so the ticking doesn't start until there's about two minutes to go.'

'But what happened?' asked Hope.

'Well, it appears that the ticking is on some sort of increased volume control. Don't ask me about the electrics. But it starts off quietly and builds up and up. Well, that's fine if it's two minutes. It does that quickly. The last couple of seconds are very loud. But of course, there was such a long span on this, and there was no sound. It was fed back into it, and was waiting for when it would go off, so it got delayed basically.'

'So, we got lucky.'

'Except for one thing, there was a phone call into the radio station not long after it, taken by the receptionist. The real bomber, we believe. He said there will be a final devastating attack that will wash away the sins of the past.'

'Doesn't sound good,' said Hope, 'but we can keep a lid on it.'

'The reason they're out there in that number and quantity,' said Macleod, pointing out to the journalists, 'is that the receptionist promptly told them. She ran out screaming and then when they arrived, she blurted it all to them.'

'Great,' said Hope.

'You think we were under the microscope before? We're

really under it now,' said Macleod.

'What's the top brass say then?'

'Those at the top wanted me to take over. I've told them no. They told me I got results last time. I told them you would have too. We need to move and find this guy fast,' said Macleod. 'From what he's saying, I think the next one could kill people, many people.'

'We got a look at him on CCTV. Ross is down there. Perry will be with him. We'll get something out of that, I think.'

'You think he's local to that area?' asked Macleod.

'I don't know. Don't know how local. But we're going to have the picture enhanced, and it will go out.'

'Two sides to that,' said Macleod. 'Keep it with us, and he doesn't know we're coming. Put it out, he'll run.'

'If we don't put it out, I don't think we'll find him. I don't think he is local. The librarian said he'd been there several times, but I think that's the point. He's going there because then if he got caught, he's miles away from where he should be. This guy is astute, knows what he's about. The way he's designing these bombs—they may be impromptu; they may be amateur looking, but they're working. This one didn't work because of interference.'

'All the other ones have worked well. The one that caught him out,' said Macleod, 'wasn't a bomb. He tried to create a bomb by using the refrigeration system.'

'Too clever for his own good, do you think?' asked Hope.

'Looks like it.'

Susan Cunningham hopped over to Hope.

'Susan, what's happening?'

'We've got problems with trying to keep the press on side. It's all gone to their latest editions, and it's out on the TV. They're asking for a statement.'

'I've got it,' said Macleod. 'You focus on getting this guy.'

Hope nodded, picked up her phone, and called Ross. 'Any luck with locals?' she asked.

'I've had the image circulated. We're currently stopping cars in the area, going out to locals on door to doors, but we're getting nothing. We need to go wide, Hope. I don't think he's local at all.'

'He's just bombed a celebrity up here, albeit a local one,' said Hope. 'He's now threatened to wash away the sins of the past. His big one is coming. I don't know how long we've got, but we need to move!'

'We need to just do it, then,' said Ross. 'Put it out to the nation. See what we get.'

Hope closed down the call and turned to Macleod.

'Press conference. Soon as. Put his image up and tell them to broadcast it. I want it across whoever, wherever, whatever papers. Online, the works. We need to know who he is.'

'Will do,' said Macleod, and walked away, phone in hand, no doubt calling the press office back at the station.

Meanwhile, Hope looked over at Susan Cunningham. She was quivering.

'Are you okay?' asked Hope, though clearly, she wasn't.

'I will be. I've got to be. You need me. It's—'

'It's what?' asked Hope.

'I went into the scene. Half the wall's down. They said they found her under half the wall. She was lucky the wall wasn't brick. It was the inside wall, but it was lying all over her legs. I saw the photographs.'

Susan reached down, her hand touching where her leg would have been, the lower part. 'It's just—'

'It's okay,' said Hope. 'If you need to go; if you need to—'

Cunningham looked up. 'After we deal with him. I can . . . I can do it. You need me. I'll get myself together.'

'Okay,' said Hope. 'Round up things here. We're putting the man's photograph up. We found it on CCTV down at Fort William's library. Maybe we'll get an address and get to move. We have to find where he's planning this last attack. We have to get there and stop him.'

Susan Cunningham nodded, then hopped away. Hope took a deep breath.

This was it. It was the calm before the storm. In half an hour, Macleod would have the picture out. They would have set up a telephone group within the main station, taking calls. Soon, hopefully, they'd have somewhere to go.

Hope thought about the fact that everyone up above would be watching. Everyone would see how she would cope with it. Macleod had turned them down, having told her, and told them, she could cope. She thought about John. She thought about the future. And then she thought about Macleod. He didn't ponder on what anybody above him thought. He didn't care.

At the moment, there were people in jeopardy. This bomber wanted people dead. That was the point. That was how Macleod got it done in all the previous cases. Don't give a toss about anyone else. 'Use the team and go save those in trouble,' Hope said to herself. 'That's how we get it done now.'

She looked through the station doors and saw Macleod addressing the press. Some of them were turning, making their way already to the station for the briefing. This was it. Final play. Within the next twenty-four hours, or maybe even forty-eight, this case will have ended, one way or another. She wouldn't let it go. She'd come out the other side.

They'll see!

Chapter 19

Hope was in her office watching the television as Macleod spoke to the press conference. He was good, clinical, and he carried a gravitas that Hope was simply stunned by. Some journalists tried to ask questions about how the investigation was going, whether they had made mistakes. Macleod cut them down. He simply said he wanted to know if anyone knew this person. The picture came up. It was grainy, but an enhanced version followed. Somebody, surely somebody would know him.

When Macleod had finished doing the press conference, Hope made her way down to the room that housed the station telephones and confidential lines. It had been expanded and there were six callers answering the phones. With them was Susan Cunningham, trying to assess what was coming in. Ross and Perry were making their way back to the station, having done all they could in Fort William.

Susan Cunningham hopped around behind the call receivers, checking over their shoulders to see what they were writing on paper. She stopped at one and then waved Hope over.

She whispered in her ear, 'Neighbour, this woman says it's a neighbour. Says it's Ian McNeil.'

'What's the address?' whispered Hope.

'Give them a moment,' said Susan. 'They'll come to it.'

Sure enough, the address was forthcoming. Susan looked at it. It was an Inverness address. Or near as darn it. Located just outside a small village. Susan turned to Hope and Hope nodded. Susan instructed the call handler to advise the woman that they were heading straight there. As she was about to leave the call room, she bumped into Macleod coming the other way.

'Got something?' he asked.

'Yes, neighbour. Got his neighbour.'

'I'm coming with you,' said Macleod.

'You sure you don't want to stop and keep an eye in case we get any more calls?'

'It's a neighbour. Neighbour doesn't call unless they're sure. Neighbour doesn't call unless—'

'They've got a vendetta against him for some reason?' said Hope.

'No,' said Macleod. 'I got the feeling about this one. It's just outside Inverness, anyway. I can come back.'

Together, the three of them made their way down to Hope's car. Once inside, they raced to the outskirts, stopping into a four-house village that was just off the A9.

Hope turned up the driveway of what was a long, winding fixture to find a woman standing on the doorstep of the cottage she clearly occupied.

'It's Ian, Ian McNeil.'

'And Ian is what? Age, description?'

'I'll take you round to his house,' she said. 'I've got a key.'

'You've got a key,' said Macleod. 'How?'

'Ian never did me any harm. Looked after each of our houses when we went away. This way,' she said, not pointing down the drive, but cutting across her lawn and going through a gap in the hedge between the houses.

The three officers followed, and soon she approached Ian's house, opening up the front door. 'He's away at the moment. Car's gone,' she said.

'What type of car is it?' asked Susan, taking out her notepad and trying to balance on her crutches as she wrote.

'Blue one,' said the woman. 'Don't know what they are. Don't do cars much. I usually get the bus.'

Great! thought Macleod but they entered the house. Inside was pristine and neat and there were photographs of the man. A family too, by the looks of it.

'He's divorced. That's his ex-wife. Although now she's dead. Couple of kids, one in New Zealand. That one's in India. And the other one there. Well, he doesn't talk to Ian.'

'So, what sort of person is he?' asked Hope.

'Ian used to be lovely,' said the woman. 'The thing is that he, well—it was after the accident.'

'What accident?'

'He was a builder. Used to do the bricks and mortar. But one day something collapsed on him. He lost a leg because of it.'

'Who'd he work for?'

'Dramness Builders.'

Macleod said quickly to Hope, 'I'll go to the builders. Get what I can from them.'

'We've only got the one car,' said Hope.

'I'll phone somebody to get you,' said Macleod, picking up his phone and disappearing. 'Keys,' he shouted. She threw the keys to him.

'You say Ian's injured?' asked Hope.

'Lost his leg. A bit like your constable there.' Cunningham looked over. 'Changes a person, doesn't it?' said the woman.

'Yes,' said Susan. 'In what way for him?'

'He was bitter about it. Very bitter about it. He didn't like the job, anyway.'

'No?' asked Hope.

'No. He was an expert back in the day.'

'An expert at what?' asked Hope.

'Demolition expert. Background in the quarries.'

'In the quarries? Do you know which ones?' asked Susan.

'Not specifically. I know he's been on the islands; he's been around Scotland, working in different places. He seemed to know the country well. But he did a bit of work with Dramness Builders when they got all this funding for projects. He was quite savvy. He's got quite a computer set up, too.'

Hope's heart was thumping. 'And have you seen him recently?'

'Been coming and going these last few weeks. Said he was out and about. But then I saw that interview. I always watch him, Macleod. He's good, isn't he? You know? That last case he did. I mean, you must think a lot of him too. Must be hard not being the boss, though. He must be good to work for.'

Hope ignored the comment and walked through the house. 'Where's the computer?' she asked.

The woman opened a door through into a study. Hope looked around. On the wall were pictures of places she recognised. There was a detailed factory schematic for the food factory. There were drawings of some sort of system. Susan peered over her shoulder.

'It's an engineering drawing,' she said. 'But it's a process drawing. My brother used to have them as a chemical engineer.

That's why it doesn't look like a proper drawing. I think that's—hang on.'

She looked at it. 'N and H? That's ammonia isn't it? NH3?'

'It's ammonia,' said Hope. 'It's him. He's the one. He planned it all. Get on the phone. Get everyone here. Now, Jona, the lot. I need Ross into this computer,' said Hope.

Cunningham turned away, picking up her phone.

'You think these bombings were him?' asked the neighbour.

'Is he capable of it?' asked Hope.

'I don't know,' said the woman. 'We talk over the fence. He gave me a lift into town a couple of times. He's a pretty nice guy but he keeps himself to himself. I've been in a few times. That's why I knew where the computer was. I had coffee with him and that, but when we talked, we talked about the gardens. He was good at that, picking out what you knew. I'd do my flowers, and he'd ask me about them.'

'Do you know if he'd received many packages recently?'

'No,' said the woman. 'No idea at all.'

'Do you know where he keeps his keys in here? I'd like to look in the garage.'

'No,' said the neighbour, 'but I know you can go through here. He showed me in here once, a while back now, kind of like a workshop. Soldering. That's what they call it, isn't it, when you do the thing on the boards? There were electronics anyway, or electrics, whatever you call them these days.'

'Show me,' said Hope. The woman led her through, but as she stepped into the garage, the woman looked bemused.

'Those boxes weren't there before.'

Hope looked and wondered. She needed Jona, and she needed her fast. She reckoned this was where he had been keeping everything. Or at least, had kept it because the boxes were empty.

* * *

Macleod strode from Hope's car to the offices of Dramness Builders. He then knocked briefly on the front door, and walked right past reception, marching upstairs. When he opened the office door of Fern Lemon, looking for Ian Lemon, there was no one inside.

'Where are you? Anyone?' shouted Macleod. A door opened down the landing, and Macleod could see Ian Lemon. Macleod's face must have looked like thunder, because Lemon was buckling.

'I want to know everything about Ian McNeil.'

Macleod strode down and saw that the two other directors for the firm, or rather pseudo-directors, were sitting in the room behind Ian Lemon.

'Have you seen my interview?' Lemon nodded. 'Sit down,' said Macleod. Lemon sat down with his brother and step-brother beside him. 'Tell me who he was. Clearly, that's what you've just been discussing.'

'Worked for us as a brickie. As far as we know, he had an accident and lost a leg. He put a claim in.'

'You pay the claim?' asked Macleod.

'He'd stepped outside of policy. He was doing things he shouldn't have been doing.'

'Truly,' said Macleod.

'That's what the foreman's report concluded,' said Clive behind him.

'Really?' said Macleod. 'Did you guys cover it up? Did you guys lose him his money? Did you squirm out of it?'

'The foreman's report said—'

Macleod slammed his fist on the table. 'The foreman's report is irrelevant. What happened?' The men looked at each other but said nothing. 'He is threatening to kill people. I need to find him. You hold information now and you'll get charged. You'll get charged with everything. Withhold the information that could prevent murder and they'll go through you. They'll lock you up and they'll throw away the key. I don't care what actually happened. I just need to know.'

'It would have bankrupted us at the time,' said Ian suddenly. 'We got out of it. We didn't have to pay.'

'And he felt, what?' asked Macleod.

'Blew the lid. But he was a man with one leg and couldn't do much. Couldn't get near us with his lawyers.'

'Looks like he might get to you in other ways. What was his background?'

'Came from the quarries, according to our notes,' said Ian Lemon.

'Anywhere else before that?' asked Macleod. 'He wasn't military, was he?'

'No, he'd worked with the quarries. Worked with explosives. And prior to that, it says here he did large-scale demolition overseas, bringing down buildings, blowing things up safely. It was irrelevant to us; we were builders. He could stick bricks together on a wall—that's all we cared about.'

Macleod swept his hands through his hair. 'I want everything, every note you've got on him, and I want it up here in the next five minutes. I want to know who he worked with. I want to speak to former colleagues. If they've left, I want their last addresses. I want everything you've got on this guy, and you'd better move quick.'

Ian Lemon's hands were shaking, and he spilled some pieces of paper. Macleod never flinched, staring at the man, until he almost ran from the office to get the information. Macleod picked up the phone and called Hope.

'He's the man. Cheated out of insurance after losing a leg.'

'I kind of guessed it was him,' said Hope. 'I'm in his workshop. There are a lot of empty boxes. Empty boxes, I think, which contained explosives. Also tech to set those explosives off. There are plans all over his office. I'm getting Ross here, Perry and Susan also, to go through all of this. We need to find the target,' she said.

'We do,' said Macleod. 'Remember what he said last time. He was true to it. This time he's going to wash away the sins of the past.'

'How do you wash away the sins of the past?'

'It's going to be targeted at these guys. I'll get addresses, I'll get where their families are, I'll get whatever,' said Macleod, 'and we'll pull it together and we'll start a manhunt.'

'We're going to need more than a manhunt, Seoras. If he's not here, and he knows we're looking for him, he'll go to ground. He's managed to get in and plant bombs with all these companies. In and out with no problems. It's going to be a grand scheme, though,' said Hope. 'It's going to be somewhere big.'

'I agree with you,' said Macleod. 'The worrying thing is, he used to do large-scale demolition. This guy could bring the house down—literally, any house.'

'We'd best move quick then,' said Hope.

Chapter 20

Hope sat in her office pouring over some details of the manhunt that was beginning in the highlands. One problem they had was they did not know where McNeil was going to carry out his final threat. It seemed it would be large-scale and now that they knew who he was, they realised he possessed the ability to carry out such a threat.

There was a banging on Hope's office door. When she said, 'Come in,' Macleod strode into the office. He didn't wait to be invited, but sat down in a seat opposite her own desk.

'Where you at?' He asked.

'I've got Perry and Susan on the manhunt. We're fanning out as much as we can. Detailed description is out there.'

'He's a one-legged man, though. It shouldn't be that difficult, should it?'

'You would think, but you never know,' said Hope. 'And if he's gone to ground, maybe he'll bide his time. Maybe he's got it in place already. Maybe he'll remotely detonate it, wherever it is.'

'Do you require any more resources?'

'It's hard,' said Hope. 'Where do you pinpoint? Where is he likely to be? We started trying to do a search, but he's taken himself deliberately somewhere. It's not a case of somebody going missing. It's a case of somebody going into hiding. Totally different. He might be nowhere near Inverness.

'We've got to look at this as probably being anywhere within the Highlands. Or the Islands. After all, it's Dramness Builders he's after.'

'But what about them? How would he target them?' asked Macleod. 'That's the real question.'

'They've got places everywhere. I've been sitting trying to get through them all. It's just location after location. And then you've got to look at how that location can be affected. There's units sent out to all their locations to check. And we're getting nothing back. Absolutely nothing. All their holdings, clean as a whistle. I've got them all going out now to check their buildings. Anything Dramness Builders were involved with.'

'Okay,' said Macleod. 'But take it easy. It's all you can do. Go through the detail. What else are you working on?'

'Boxes in his house. Going through the computer, along with Jona. She's confirmed that the empty boxes we found had been labelled up with explosives. And the explosives are not there.'

'He must have had something big to carry them, no?' asked Macleod.

'If he took it all in one go, yes, he would.'

'Think about it. He's also got to set them. He's not exactly that mobile, is he?' said Macleod.

'You've seen Susan, haven't you? She's very mobile, despite losing her leg. And it hasn't stopped him so far.'

'What I'm saying is, if he's going to plant all of this, and you have to place explosives carefully, it's going to take a bit of time. Is he doing trips backwards and forwards?'

'I understand what you're getting at, but we're so behind the curve on this, Seoras. We've no idea where he wants to go or how he's going to do it.'

'We know he was a demolition expert,' said Macleod. 'It's in his past—the answer. We know he could set explosives to bring anything down safely. This got me thinking. If he's going to harm Dramness Builders, he'll look to harm them specifically. Through all of this, he hasn't looked to kill anyone else. He made a mistake with the first one. He over-complicated the situation, went away from what he knew. Tried to make it happen off a system he didn't really understand. Hence, the explosion happened. Killed someone. He'd be doubly sure this time he'd get the right people.'

'But how does he get them? They're aware now. I know what you're saying, Seoras. But it doesn't take away from the fact that they're who he'll go for.'

'Do you really know what I'm thinking? Do you know where they all live?'

'Yes, they live on a load of new builds that the company was involved with. It's about an hour outside of Inverness. There's a big hydro structure down the valley from it.'

'I think I know it,' said Macleod. 'Nice place. They're obviously making enough money.'

'I've got units down there. Uniforms covering it all. They're not seeing anything. Places have been searched. We brought in some help from the army. People who understand the bombs and got Jona talking to them. We reckon he'll set it off with quite a simple device, too.'

Macleod stood up. 'Anything you need, say to me—okay? I'm going to go do the press conference.'

'What are you telling them?'

'Putting the photo up again. Anyone sees this man, call it in. The usual.'

'Jona was going through the garage, trying to see if there was any mud or anything that could have come from somewhere. Try to trace it, anything unusual.'

'It's one of those cases,' said Macleod. 'You're waiting for the break; you're waiting for it to come to you. You've got to look the other way, actually think about where it's going to happen, be ahead of him, guess his game.'

'Any help you can throw in,' said Hope, 'would be more than welcome.'

'Well, if I get any ideas, . . .' said Macleod.

He turned and walked out of the office. Hope thought she could see the strain on him. No wonder! Hope was feeling the strain herself. She had to text John, tell him she was knee deep, and not to disturb her unless it was critical. She hated doing that, blocking him out. But she had to do it, because she needed to think. Hope had to get on top of this.

* * *

Susan Cunningham hopped along with her crutches and arrived at the roadblock that had been set up on the road outside of Inverness. Cars were being pulled over and quickly asked if they had seen anything of Ian McNeil. His picture was held up. Despite the disgruntlement of several drivers at having their journeys interrupted, Susan thought it might actually get some results.

'Anything yet?' asked Perry.

'No,' said Susan. 'How hard can it be to spot a one-legged man?'

'Busy one-legged at the moment, though. Might have a prosthetic.'

'Ross is looking into his medical history. Hopefully, we'll have a lot more on him soon,' said Susan. As she said that, she was called from two cars over by one of the constables. Susan skirted around two other cars that were also being questioned and saw a woman in the front seat of a car with some kids in the rear.

'This lady believes she may have seen him.'

Susan acknowledged the constable and turned to the lady. 'Where?'

'Back up the road, there's a coffee shop,' she said. 'It's a bit back. We stopped in. I'm not from the area, but there was a one-legged man there. I was seeing him from behind, but I think that's him.'

Susan nodded, then asked the woman for further details on where the coffee shop was. Pulling up a map on her phone, Susan traced it back and realised exactly where she was talking about.

'Perry, let's go,' she said, advising a couple of constables to follow in police cars, Susan jumped into Perry's car. Susan was driven by Perry back along the road until they got close to the coffee shop the woman had talked about.

'Take it easy,' said Susan.

Perry parked up a distance away so that no one in the coffee shop could actually see him. Susan got out of the car and scooted along with her crutches towards the edge of the coffee shop.

'I'll go inside,' she said. 'If he's not alerted, it might be easier to grab him that way.'

'I'll cover the door,' said Perry. 'I'll get our constables to flank.'

'Make sure they're not seen,' she said.

Susan hopped up the steps. It was arduous taking the steps, trying to co-ordinate your hands while still being on your crutches, but it was giving the impression she wasn't looking for anyone. She was struggling enough with her own issues.

She stepped inside the coffee shop and initially looked up towards the counter; after all, that's what most people would do. She hobbled over, asked for a coffee, and one bun neatly displayed at the side. Hobbling back, she sat down at a table in the corner. She glanced around as she took out her mobile phone.

Over in the far corner, she could see a man, but when she looked at his chair, she saw only one leg protruding from his body. The other side of the trouser had been neatly sewn up.

Susan texted Perry saying he was there. One problem was the man had a cap sitting across his face. Of course, it made perfect sense it was Ian McNeil. He'd been trying to keep out of sight. Size-wise, he fitted the description. But Susan just wasn't sure.

The coffee arrived, along with the bun, and she calmly ate. She ate and drank, waiting for the man to turn. However, he didn't. There was a paper in front of him, and he was scanning every bit.

With her bun complete, Susan decided she couldn't wait any longer. She stood up and hobbled across to him.

'Excuse me, if I could just have a word,' said Susan. Her right hand was in her back pocket, and she had handcuffs ready.

'I'm sorry,' said the man. He didn't look up.

'I was wondering if you could help me.'

The man glanced across at her legs, but his head never raised.

'Same as me,' he said. 'How did you lose yours?'

'Wall fell on me,' said Susan.

'I lost mine in the workplace. Lost a lot with it,' he said. 'Too much.'

Susan sat down in the chair opposite. 'Well, my name's Susan Cunningham. How are you doing?'

The man looked up. 'I'm getting by,' he said.

Susan stared into his face. This wasn't Ian McNeil. Her heart sank for a moment, annoyed that they'd been down here wasting their time. But she continued to talk to the man for another few moments before grabbing her crutches and hobbling back out. As she came down the steps, Perry raced over to help her. But her mind was miles away.

'What?' said Perry.

'It's not him. Yes, he's got one leg. Yes, he might have been our guy, but he's not. Looks absolutely nothing like the photograph. In fact,' she said, 'his name's Jim. Or rather, James.'

'Back to the car, then,' said Perry. 'Back to the car. It is a needle in a haystack, though, isn't it?'

'What's that?' asked Susan, miles away.

'Needle in a big haystack. But we need to keep searching.'

'You think we'll find them this way,' said Susan. 'I'm not convinced.'

'Of course you're not convinced. None of us are convinced,' said Perry. 'But you keep going.'

'Do you know something though, Perry? I get him. If that had happened to me and people didn't care, if people tried to diddle me out of what I was due, after I got hurt in their workplace, I would be angry. I would be raging.'

'You wouldn't blow people up, though.'

'Who's to say?' spat Susan. 'The first one was an accident. He's only looking to blow up those who hurt him.'

'Doesn't matter, though, does it? If that's what it does to you, it's hurt you more than losing the leg ever did.'

Susan nodded. 'Come on. Back to the grind,' she said.

Chapter 21

Hope sat looking at her paperwork in front of her. She had sketches, drawings, pen on paper trying to get into her head where this guy was going to strike. She talked to Ross on the phone. He was still breaking into the computer. The man obviously had some tech knowledge, but Ross was confident they could get into the inner pieces soon enough. He had gone into depth on the man's history, and all that had done for Hope was to tell her McNeil really could blow something up.

They'd also found McNeil's truck, which was really worrying Hope. The truck would have been used to move the explosives. It was only a small Bedford-type truck, and they had put out a description of it, trying to track its movements, and they found it quickly in a car park in the forest. But if he'd given it up, it meant he didn't need it anymore. It meant everything was in place.

Jona was still working through the house as well. The Asian woman had sent over pictures of everything on the wall, and Hope was working her way through them. She'd gone for the obvious and realised that the drawings she was looking at had been schematics of the places he'd already bombed.

An email arrived on Hope's computer, and she tapped on the keyboard, opening it up.

'Found these in the bin. I've lifted them for evidence, but took photographs first. Wondered if they might be of any use.'

Hope loaded the photographs. There was scrumped-up paper, which when laid out flat, contained a series of lines. They looked like rough, technical sketches. There wasn't a lot written on them, but Hope could see the wavy lines. She surmised there was a drop into water. She could see that there was an enormous face to the side of whatever it was.

Hope ran a copy off on the printer and placed it down on her desk. She looked around the various sites that Dramness Builders had been involved in and was struggling to match any up. The buildings that they created, none of them looked like this. Then again, it was such a rough sketch, how would you know?

There was a ring in the bottom left-hand corner of the paper. Water was above it and those large flat lines sliding up somewhere. Hope stood up and turned to look out the window.

There were no press there, unlike at the front of the building. She breathed in deeply, and then something struck her.

She turned back and looked at the shape of the ring that was drawn. It was like something. She hoked through the papers before her. And then she came up with the shape that she'd recognised. It was the estate that the families of the Dramness Builders' owners lived on.

It was a crude drawing, but it fitted the outline. Coincidence, though? She didn't believe in coincidences, so she kept at it. What else was on that paper? Water. She pulled out the map; there was the Hydro Dam, and there was the water that ran from it

She needed to talk to somebody about this. She placed a call into the Water Services Department at the council, asking for someone who would understand that dam. They passed her along, until eventually, she got to the architect who had designed the dam.

'Hello,' he said, 'my name's Douglas. I've been told that you want some information about one of the dams I designed.'

'My name's Detective Inspector Hope McGrath. I've got an issue at the moment. You've probably seen it in the news. We've had a lot of bombings and I'm worried about this dam. You say you built it.'

'Well, yes. Designed it. Didn't build it.'

'Were Dramness Builders involved in it?' asked Hope.

'Not at all,' said the man. 'They're not capable of that sort of build.'

'What's the purpose of it?' asked Hope.

'The purpose of any dam is to stop water.'

'Why would you stop water in that particular place?'

'There were plans for the plain down below it,' said Douglas, 'to be used to build housing. I believe they have done. So, we had to hold back the water. It took a while for the land to dry out, but then we had made a residential valley out of it.'

'What would happen if that dam came down?'

'Excuse me? What do you mean, down?' said an alarmed Douglas.

'What if somebody blew that dam up?' asked Hope. 'Is there enough water there to do significant damage?'

'You certainly would have a major problem. The houses down below, they're probably actually below the level the water would have been at previously. With a significant break, you would flood the water onto everywhere down there.'

'And how fast do you think it would get down there?' asked Hope.

'Well it would shift. It would really shift. The volumes we're talking about. I think . . . well, if you had no warning, you'd be lucky to get everybody out. Extremely lucky. Many people in those houses wouldn't be alive.'

'Thank you,' said Hope. She put down the phone and placed a call to Macleod.

'It's where?' he said when she told him.

'Hydroelectric dam. Plain below, it would take it all out. It's where the houses are of Dramness Builders' directors are.'

'Go,' said Macleod. 'Everything, throw everything at it.'

Hope called down for uniform officers and started to get things under way. She wondered about racing in, though. Would the man see them? Would he then just blow everything up? Instead, Hope decided to enter quietly, scan the dam, get a team together to find the man, and have uniform ready below if needs be.

Hope called Susan Cunningham and Perry, and told them to meet her, along with Ross, close to the dam. As she made her way down the steps towards the rear car park, she saw the Assistant Chief Constable coming towards her.

'Are you sure about this?' he said.

'Sure as we can be. Evidence points that way. Pointing nowhere else,' said Hope.

'Be very careful,' said Jim. 'You might end up making him explode his devices prematurely. Could be a lot of lives at stake.'

'That's why I'm trying to go in silent. I'm going out the back door. Don't come with me,' said Hope. 'Press will know something's up.'

Hope walked down to her car. She felt the eyes of Jim on her back and was aware that she was being judged. Was Macleod always being judged? She remembered when he was the DI, and he talked about those above him. Fortunately, Macleod didn't judge her, but Jim could. He always wanted results, and this could go wrong catastrophically.

Hoped made her way out to the car, jumped in, and stopped for a moment before turning on the engine. *But there's nothing for it,* she thought. *You have to follow your instincts. Go with it. It's not like Macleod's never not got it wrong. But he always gets it right in the end.*

The trip out to the dam took about half an hour. As she arrived, in a lay-by in the road, some five hundred metres from the dam, she saw Ross's car already there. Shortly after that, Perry and Susan turned up. Hope pulled them all together in the lay-by.

'We're going to slip up, look like we're ordinary people. Apparently, there's one control point at the dam, a single building on top. He must have planted everything already.'

'How?' asked Susan Cunningham.

'He's used to planting explosives,' said Hope. 'He'll have been used to possibly working zip wires and climbing gear. He knows how to plant things in the right place and he may have been doing this for a while. Possibly at night.'

'So,' said Ross. 'How do we do it? We're all going to be on one side, working across it.'

'We will,' said Hope. 'Come on. You and I go first, Ross. Susan and Perry can pick up this side, in case he's about and makes a run for it.'

Driving the cars the last half kilometre, they stopped in a

small car park at the side of the dam. People would walk over it sometimes for the view. It wasn't a large tourist attraction, but it was somewhere that a few people came to enjoy the highland scenery. It was certainly a breathtaking view down from the dam. As she stepped out, feeling the wind blowing, Hope realised it wasn't that cold a day.

The breeze was warm, but she could see no one on top of the dam. There was a concrete structure about halfway across, and with Ross in tow, she made her way towards it. As she got there, she could see a window and looked in. She could see some control panels for the dam, but this was locked. However, there was clearly no one inside. She continued with Ross to the far side of the dam.

'Where is he then?' asked Ross.

'He might not be here. He might hide out to come to it later,' said Hope.

'So, what do we do?' asked Ross.

'Wait, give me a minute,' she said. Hope walked to the edge of the dam and looked down beyond it. 'How do you plant explosives in here?' asked Hope.

'Well, I don't know,' said Ross. 'I can't see anything on the outside, so I'm scanning the surface of the dam. Can you get inside that control unit? Does it go down?'

'Not as far as I'm aware,' she said. 'I'll call and see, but I'm going to check the outside structure.'

'How are you going to check the outside structure?' asked Ross. 'You're not going over that wall and down.'

'No,' said Hope, 'but I'll go down the side of it, down along the grass where it's built into the mountainside.'

Hope walked down to where the concrete met the soil. It was steep, and she had to be careful, before she suddenly threw herself back onto her backside.

'Careful,' said Ross, 'you don't know how far you'll fall if you take a tumble.'

'I'm not going too far down,' she said. The dam wasn't quite sheer, but it was a steep incline. Hope lay down on it, and slowly clambered across the dam.

'What are you doing?' shouted Ross.

'I need to see if he's been tampering with anything.'

As she moved herself across the dam, lying with her face to it, entrusting her boots to grip tight enough so she didn't slide, it reminded her of being a girl on a roof. But this was a steep roof.

'Are you getting anything?' asked Ross.

Hope ignored him, moving her hand out and running it across the surface. *That felt strange,* she thought. She clambered across and looked at what could have been a repair on the dam. *What was it? A break in,* she thought. *Did he break into the surface and put something there and cover it up again? You could do that, couldn't you?*

Hope scratched at the concrete with her hands, but she wasn't going to dig into it. It did look like a repair, though. That wasn't the original stone. It had been filled, packed back.

'I said, have you got anything?' asked Ross.

'Possibly,' said Hope. She took out her phone, and took a photograph.

This could be it, she thought. She felt tense, very tense, because if it was, she was lying on the edge of a dam with explosives inside it, and the man on the trigger was nowhere in sight. She tried to see if there was anything further along the wall. *You'd do it at the same height, wouldn't you?* she thought. Then she realised she knew nothing about explosives, and she didn't know how they'd built the dam, and where he would put the bombs in.

'I think you should come back,' said Ross.

That doesn't make any sense. Hope ignored him, sliding her way out further. *Was that another one she saw? Surely . . .*

An almighty explosion ripped the air. For a moment, Hope's heart pounded. But the dam was intact. Completely intact.

'My goodness,' said Ross. 'It's from the valley.'

Hope immediately worked her way back towards the edge. She could feel her phone vibrating now as she began to run up the side of the hill. It was steep. She had to be careful she didn't trip and slide back down.

When she got to the top, she pulled out her phone, but Ross was already shouting at her. 'A bomb's gone off down there. It's in a civic centre down in the community.'

'Is anyone—'

'No,' said Ross. 'Don't believe so, at least they haven't said so.'

'Quickly!'

Hope ran across the dam, Ross in tow. When she got to the other side, she saw Perry with Susan Cunningham.

'Hope,' said Susan. 'They just called up. Apparently, he's taken out half a building. A couple of people injured. Looks like he's messed it up. Looks like—'

'Are there more devices down there?' butted in Ross.

'I don't know what they're saying,' said Susan. 'It's bedlam.'

'Let's get there,' said Hope. As she ran for the car, her thoughts went back to Jim, the Assistant Chief Constable. He told her she needed to be right. Well, she was wrong. And now she was going to face the music. And possibly the injured, or maybe even the dead.

Chapter 22

Hope arrived down in the valley beneath the dam. As she drove on to the cultured estate there were fire engines racing to the scene. Ambulances were arriving, too. There was chaos to a large degree, uniformed police officers trying to make a cordon to keep people back. The press, of course, were as quick as a flash in arriving too.

Hope parked the car a little distance from the civic centre. It was clear where it was because of the utter confusion surrounding it. People were out of their houses, running to see what was going on.

Hope's phone rang. She picked it up, putting it to her ear and cupping a hand over her other ear so she could hear it.

'Hope, what's going on? Did you have anything? Anything to say he'd do this?' It was Macleod.

'No,' she said. 'This makes little sense. I don't remember the civic centre being on the list. I've gone over all of that list, Seoras. I've checked them all, but it's not there. I'm sure of it. I need to get back to the office.'

'Is it on your desk?' asked Macleod. 'I'm in the station.'

'Yes, it'll be on my desk. The full list is on my desk.'

'I'll call you back,' said Macleod. Hope closed the call and watched as the uniforms in front of her took charge.

'You got a sergeant with you?' Hope asked.

'No,' said one constable. Hope turned to Ross. 'Get on this. Get a perimeter set up. Find out from me who's injured, who isn't.'

She turned and looked away for a moment. Someone came up with a camera, right in her face. She went to turn away, but suddenly a microphone was stuffed before her.

'Detective Inspector McGrath. Have you failed to spot this? Is this the end? How many people are dead?'

'We're only just on scene,' said Hope. 'If you'll excuse me, we are kind of busy.'

She turned and walked away, right past one of the uniformed constables, whispering in the woman's ear, 'Keep them away. Back as far as you can.' She heard Susan Cunningham hopping after her.

'You and Perry. See Ross and help out here. Susan, find out for me what happened. How many people have been injured? Was the Civic Centre occupied? Were there people about? Get me the detail.'

Susan nodded, but Hope could see the shock on her face. None of them had seen this coming. None of them had seen the fact that the dam wasn't the right place. Standing behind the cordon, Hope felt useless.

As she stood there, she could see more police cars arriving. Worse than that, she saw a police car coming that she recognised, and not one she wanted to see. The Assistant Chief Commissioner stepped out and was spoken to by Ross. Hope moved off in a different direction. She needed time to think. All she'd get from him was a lambasting. He'd come and question her on why she hadn't seen this, why she hadn't covered it off.

The phone rang again, and she answered it.

'Hope, it's Seoras, it's not one of their buildings,' he said. 'It's not one of their buildings. Don't believe they did any work on it at all,' he said.

'Are you thinking what I'm thinking, Seoras?' asked Hope.

'Tell me what you're thinking.'

'This isn't right. It's certainly not the end.'

'Where do those drawings come from? The ones you said made you think it was the dam.'

'Found in his bin. In his house. Jona found them.'

'You got a copy?'

'They're in the files. On the case files. Look for them in there. Jona uploaded them.'

'Hold the line,' said Macleod.

Hope stared around her. There was a woman on the floor, blood pouring from the side of her face. A paramedic was there, attending to her. A young child was walking around, lost. A constable was taking hold of him, trying to find his mother. It was still dusty in the air. This wasn't like a lot of the other explosions. They were smaller. This was . . .

What was it? thought Hope. *What was it like? The impact wasn't strong, though.* She looked around. Grand finale? This was no grand finale. This was barely a small curtain call. She went closer towards the Civic Building but then someone stopped her.

'I wouldn't go in there, Inspector. It's not safe.'

'Is there anyone in, though?' asked Hope.

'Don't know. Fire brigade are going to make an entry soon but they need to make sure it's safe.'

'Get those people back' shouted a voice. Hope looked over.

It was the Senior Fire Chief on scene denoted by the vest he was wearing. Hope stepped back. As she did so, she felt a tap on the shoulder. She turned into the face of the assistant chief constable.

'How did we miss this?'

'We missed this,' said Hope, 'because it's not right. This is wrong.'

'What do you mean by that?' asked Jim.

'It's not one of their buildings. They have done no work on it.'

'But he stuck a bomb in it,' said Jim. 'Look. Look around you. How on earth did we miss this?'

'Grand finale,' said Hope, almost absent-mindedly. She could hear a voice, a quiet voice, coming from the other side, from somewhere.

'I'm speaking to you, Detective Inspector.'

'One moment,' said Hope. She put her finger up in front of the assistant chief constable. It wasn't something that made him happy.

'Go ahead, Seoras,' she said to the phone.

'There's definitely water on it. And the big circle at the bottom, with the few lines in it. That circle was the one that you matched up, yes?' asked Macleod.

'Matched up to the community at the bottom.'

'Talk to me. When you're up at the dam,' said Macleod, 'did you see anything?'

'I think. Well, I don't know,' said Hope. 'There were repairs on the wall. Repairs in the dam wall. I mean, there could have been repairs.'

'Who's that?' said a voice in the background.

'What's going on?' asked Macleod.

'Assistant Chief Constable's here.'

'Is that Macleod?' said Jim. 'Give me that phone.'

He grabbed the phone off Hope. A tirade was beginning but Hope was staring back up towards the dam. She looked around. She raised her hand when she saw Perry and waved him towards her.

'Perry, where are the families of Dramness Builders at the minute?'

'I'll find out for you,' he said, and disappeared. She turned back to the assistant chief constable, but he was still giving Macleod an earful.

'Can I have that back?' Hope said to him.

Jim's face was thunderous. 'I am talking to your boss. I am—'

'I need to talk to my boss,' said Hope, 'now!'

'When I'm done.'

Susan Cunningham was walking past at the same time, clearly trying to make a detour so as not to get into the middle of what was turning into a serious fracas. But Hope grabbed her.

'Give me your phone.'

'My phone?' said a bemused Susan. 'Here.' Hope looked down the phone's contacts list and pressed the number for her own office.

'You just ignore that phone,' said Jim. 'Seoras, you hear me?'

'Hope,' said Macleod, from the other end of Susan's phone. 'What?'

'The families of the Dramness Builders, their houses are on this estate. If they are in their houses?'

'Well, if they are,' said Macleod, 'they're not going to leave at the moment, are they?'

'No,' said Hope, 'because everyone thinks this is the scene.

Everyone thinks the bomb's been done. So, they're going to keep them in their house because they don't want to come out into this. They don't want to come out into the press and the chaos.'

'Are you talking to him on that phone?' cried Jim. 'Macleod! Macleod! Give me that phone.'

Hope snatched the phone away from Jim, turned and began to walk.

'I've got Perry checking that out. But if so, McNeil will have them inside. He'll have everybody else here. And if he can blow that dam, he'll have a grand finale.'

'I'm on my way,' said Macleod. Macleod closed the call from his end.

'He's not there. He just closed the call,' cried Jim. 'McGrath, come here!'

Hope handed Cunningham's phone back to her. 'Can I have my phone, please? And it's Hope. I believe we're meant to be on first-name terms at the moment.'

'Don't you speak to me like that?'

Hope was always professional. Always toeing the line. But this wasn't right. Lives were at stake.

'I want you back to the station now!' thundered Jim. 'You'll type up a full report on how this came about. I want to know everything. I want to keep away from that press corps. And where's Macleod?'

'Macleod's on his way,' said Hope. 'Seoras is coming.'

'Would you stop staring at that damn fixture up there?'

But Hope was looking at the dam. Someone ran up behind her and she turned to see Perry.

'When the explosion went off, they stayed here. They're inside the houses. We've got a police guard around them.'

'Really?' said Hope.

'That's good though, isn't it?' said Perry. 'I mean, keep the press away from them. Keeps the bomber going to them and when he realises they weren't there.'

'McGrath, you need to be going to the office now. I want that report.' Jim was raging.

Hope continued looking up at the dam. 'Perry,' she said, 'do you think this is a distraction?'

'Distraction,' he said. 'Why?'

'Don't play games,' said the assistant chief constable. 'You start walking or your job will be on the line.'

'Perry, I asked you a question,' said Hope. 'Do you think this is a distraction? All this, a distraction. That building, it isn't part of any job they've done.'

'Isn't part of any job they've done,' mused Perry.

'It doesn't fit the bill. And why blow it up? What's the grand finale?' said Hope. 'He's gone for nobody else. He's tried not to kill anyone innocent. He stuffed it up at the start.'

'You don't know that,' said Jim. 'Get me the report so I can work this out.'

Hope put her hand up in Jim's face. 'Enough,' she said. 'Perry, you hearing me. What do you say?'

Perry was motionless, the mind whirring. 'Damn, Hope,' said Perry, 'they said they would sweep everything, didn't they?'

'Yes,' said Hope.

'We need to go,' said Perry. 'We need to go!'

'You're going nowhere,' shouted Jim. 'And you, Detective Constable Perry, you will stand here and get on with your job in assisting.'

Hope walked off. 'Perry, round up the team. Get Ross, tell him what's happened. Tell him what I think.'

'You're doing no such thing, Constable Perry. You'll escort Detective Inspector McGrath back to the office, where she will write out a report for me on everything that's happened.'

There was a rage building inside of Hope. He couldn't do it. They'd chased her off the last case. But Macleod hadn't. Seoras was on his way. Perry said she was right. This wasn't her line of attack normally. This wasn't the way she thought. She'd probably surprised herself in coming up with the notion. But she was right. She was flaming right.

'Detective Inspector!' A hand went onto her shoulder. Hope swept an arm round, knocking the hand away.

'Get your hands off me,' said Hope. 'I've got lives to save.'

She strode off towards the police cordon. As she stepped through, the press gathered towards her. But she ignored the comments, ignored the half accusations of getting things wrong and strode towards her car. Climbing inside, Hope turned on the engine and drove away. She prayed she wasn't too late. Could McNeil still be stopped?

Chapter 23

Hope drove up to the dam, her hands shaking on the wheel. She'd basically told Jim, the assistant chief constable, to stuff it, and ignored his instructions. She'd better be right. But something else was growing within Hope. As she drove up, she thought about John.

And she thought about the life they could have. They both wanted a child. They were both keen to have a child. Did detective work really sit with having a child? She'd have to have it on her terms. The child would have to have time. Mum would have to be there.

Something inside Hope was changing. She realised the job was not everything. Macleod had always said that. The job wasn't everything! The people in the job were everything. At the moment, those people were about to die in the village below, in the melee of the aftermath of an explosion. An explosion that made no sense. Every other explosion had made sense.

What's the worst they can do, she thought. *Sack me. It wouldn't be half as bad as sitting back in the station, as the dam blew and tonnes of water came charging down, killing however many.*

And Seoras was on his way.

She didn't realise before just how much she relied on his opinion, how much she really trusted it. But Perry was with her, too. She wasn't the one to see things through that way. She wasn't the one to understand that line of thought. Perry had come to an answer almost instantly. Just a few moments of thought and contemplation.

As Hope pulled up in the small car park, her heart was beating fast. She'd be about to step out onto somewhere where there could be explosives under her feet. But where was he then? Surely, he'd have to detonate it from a sensible distance. But if he wanted to see and make sure of what would happen, the best place to see the devastation would be up on the dam.

As Hope parked, she realised there was another car. Stepping out of her car, she quietly made her way over to the other one. She looked inside. An automatic. *Is that how he would drive? Did amputees use automatics?*

So, Ian McNeil was probably here. Here to watch. But where?

She tried to stay low while she approached the dam but all there was on the dam was the control room. On the other side was just more dam. There was no sign from the vehicle that he brought anything else with him. Nothing to say the bombs hadn't been planted earlier.

Hope walked up on top of the dam, slowly making her way across. She looked down at the side at one point. She gulped at the large drop and then stared at the river that flowed into the valley.

On her right-hand side, she saw the vast lake of water as she got close to the control room. The door was open. Slowly, she walked over. Inside, Hope could see Ian McNeil and he was holding a detonator. Ian McNeill smiled at her as she reached the room.

'I wondered if anybody would know,' he said. 'You found me, eventually. I guess that was well done.'

'Did you want to be found?' asked Hope.

'Maybe.'

He had two legs, from what Hope could see, presumably a prosthetic. In his hand, he held a small gun and was pointing it at Hope. There was a device in his hand which Hope had presumed was the detonator.

'What are the explosives?' asked Hope.

'You tell me. You had a good look at one. They're in the dam.'

'You've gone down and put them in the dam.'

'Took a while working at night. People think you lose a leg and you can't do things. I can, and I did.'

'So you're going to blow the dam,' said Hope. 'The water's going to rush down and, from your point of view, hopefully kill a lot of the Dramness management.'

'I wondered if anybody would understand what I was going to do. When you got to me, I had to leave the house quickly, but I thought I'd covered everything from the dam, and then I remembered, I didn't empty the bin, did I?'

'We found some sketches,' said Hope. 'I was able to put two and two together. You'd drawn the town quite accurately, the shape of it at least.'

'You have to be accurate when you're a demolition expert. You must be accurate, with the amount of explosives placed here and there. I had to do the research. I binned it all, or got rid of it, except for that one piece of paper, because I didn't like the way I'd drawn the damn walls. I didn't want you to know about this one. The others were fine, though. I wasn't looking to kill anyone with the others. I wanted to get my story out.'

'Can I come in?' asked Hope. Ian nodded, and she stepped inside. The control room had a simple control desk. On her left it showed different pumps and valves that could be opened. Ian was sitting in the chair that accompanied that panel, but he had pushed it back against the rear wall.

'One thing I don't understand,' said Hope, 'is why you are here? You can surely explode this from elsewhere, even from the car park. You're not going to be bringing it in as well, are you?'

'No,' said Ian. 'When the charges go, it'll just be the dam wall that breaks, enough to then send all the water down and it'll take those bastards out.'

'It'll take everybody else out with it, too,' said Hope.

'That estate down there, you know it's . . . it's built by them.'

'What do you mean?' asked Hope.

'It's built by people who, well, use other people. Use them to make money, then they buy themselves a nice place to live away from everyone, while the rest of us suffer. Do you know what it's like to lose a leg?'

'I don't,' said Hope, 'but one of my team does. She lost a leg recently, well, just below the knee,'

'And what did you do for her?'

'We've offered her the best that we can. We've offered her psychologists. We've offered her a health medical, time off.'

'Well, that's to your credit,' said Ian. 'I was offered nothing. In fact, the payout—they blocked it. They stopped it. Will you block the payout?'

'I don't know the detail of the payout she'll get. But they won't block it. She lost it in the line of saving someone else. From a bomb, funnily enough,' said Hope.

'I used to explode things. I used to bring them down safely so nobody would get hurt. You learn an awful lot. Worked overseas and then hit hard times when I lost my job. Became a brickie. I wasn't that good at being a brickie. Yes, I was okay, but it wasn't great. They cut corners though. Dramness builders cut corners, which caused me problems.

'Because something fell on me one day and I lost a leg. Not below the knee, but right from the top. You sometimes feel the pain from it. Do you know that?' he said. 'You feel pain. It's not there and you feel pain. And you mourn it. It's part of you. I know that sounds obvious but you don't realise how much things are of you until you lose them.'

'What went wrong with the first explosion?' asked Hope.

'I got that wrong. That's what I did. I got that completely wrong. I thought I could engineer the system. I thought, let's be clever, make an effective explosion, because that would then lead you away from me. You see, I wanted the world to be ready. I wanted the world to see what was about to happen. If I wasn't using explosives, you wouldn't come looking for me. You wouldn't trace it to my previous job, but now you have. I knew it was a risk.'

'Why are you up here, though?' said Hope. 'Why are you sitting on top of the very thing that's going to explode?'

'You're right, of course. I'm not *that good* with explosives, and I couldn't guarantee that this little station in the middle would stay intact. It'll probably go down there as well. But I deserve that.'

'Because?' asked Hope.

'Well, because of the first one. I didn't mean to kill that shift manager. Just me being clever and not understanding systems. That's why I went back to my explosives, what I did understand. Explosives. This stuff in this dam, much more advanced than the other things I used. But I know them all. I know how to use them. I know what to do with them. And that's what I'm going to do.

'But you were just doing your job. You can walk,' said Ian. 'You can walk back there, to the car park. Tell them you didn't get to me in time. They'll not blame you.'

'I'm afraid they will blame me,' said Hope. 'They'll definitely blame me. You see, sometimes things don't work for us either. You let off all these bombs, the press expects us to be on it. Flood down there and we're expected to stop you. Expected to see your ploy. I've just got told off for coming up here. I got told to go to the office, do a report, to say how I'd messed up, and yet here I am, right with you, the man at the centre.'

Hope was wondering how long she could string this out. Perry was going to come, Macleod would come. She'd get help, but help was going to be over her shoulder, and he could see that. All he had to do was press a button. That was it. She could try to grab the detonator, but at the moment, he was pointing a gun at her. It wouldn't take a lot for him to fire it.

She needed him to move, needed him to do something that took him out of his comfortable position.

'You won't be able to see it. You won't be able to see from here.'

'What do you mean?' asked Ian.

'You won't be able to see. When it all explodes and you charge down the hill, all the water pouring out from underneath you as you fall into it, you'll just be at the back. You won't get that thrill.'

'Suppose you're right,' he said. 'It would be better to be up the front, wouldn't it? I'll readjust,' he said. 'But you walk.

Walk for me. You look like a woman who has someone. I don't want them to suffer.'

She was sweating buckets. The evening was warm, but more than that, the tension was palpable. Ian stood up from his chair. He was going to turn it around, but he was struggling to do everything at once. The leg obviously bothered him.

'Make your way,' he said,

'I'm just going to take my coat off,' she said, 'sweat dripping in my eyes.'

'Okay,' the man nodded.

Hope undid her jacket, but not too slowly. She wanted to make a sudden move, but sudden moves stick out more when you've stopped moving, or you're moving so slowly they're really obvious. Instead, she undid one arm from the coat, and then on the other hand, just as the coat was dropping off the other arm, she grabbed it and flung it straight at Ian's face.

Hope dived to the right, and Ian fired, a bullet ricocheting past her, careering up into the control panel room. Hope snatched the trigger device and tried to kick Ian hard in the leg, but it was his prosthetic, and she simply bounced back away from him.

She saw him go to fire the gun at her, hauling her coat off. It had a hole in the bottom where the first bullet had passed through. As she turned to run away, she lashed out with her hand. Hope managed to push the gun to the right-hand side, and he let go a shot that went straight through the window of the control room. Hope stepped outside quickly, slamming the door behind her.

She turned left around the back of the control room and sprinted to the far side of the dam. If she had gone straight to her car, he could have opened the door and shot her in the back. He would have to follow her for the detonator. He would have to come round.

There was a cry of rage from inside. As Hope sprinted along the top of the dam. She saw no path out. She would have to go onto the mountainside and, having been down there earlier, she knew how steep that was.

Chapter 24

Hope McGrath ran for her life, the detonation device in her hand. She wasn't looking at it, just picking her feet up, driving as hard as she could. If she thought she was sweating before, she was truly sweating now. Hope wondered how long it would take for McNeil to get out of the control room and then be facing her. She would have her back to him, so she couldn't know.

She started off running in a straight line. Hope wondered if, by the time she got closer to the end, should she be zigzagging? It would give him a more difficult target. Maybe by that point, he would be out and ready to shoot. She pondered this in her mind and then began her zigzags. A few seconds later, she heard the gunfire.

Her heart skipped a beat, but it was still beating a few seconds later, so he must have missed. Somewhere on the mountainside ahead of her was a bullet. She continued to zigzag, this time something skimmed off the floor by her foot. Hope was now at the end of the dam, and slid round a concrete post out to the grass. She could go right, she thought. That would take her down to the water, the lake behind the dam. But there was a steep drop, and it was vertically down. If she went down the front side of the dam where the river flowed from it, she could at least scrabble about.

Could she go up, though? Possibly. But she'd be on the mountainside, and she couldn't get up that high that quick. It wouldn't be long before he would be there, ready to pick her off with the gun.

There were no options. Hope scrambled down where she'd gone before; only this time, she was doing it at speed.

Hope flipped herself over and let her feet fall down the steep slope. Every now and again she'd touch her foot in, trying to put brakes on her descent.

He was shooting again, from the top of the dam. As he ran along, he wasn't that quick, clearly the prosthetic causing him an issue. But he moved. It wouldn't be a case of Hope simply outrunning him. Besides, where was she going to run to? With her hands up above her and her feet below, she was descending at a rapid rate down the hillside. However, as she looked down, she saw a problem looming.

Further down the dam, the hillside cut in and produced a slope she'd be able to stand on. It was just that beyond that slope was sheer. Hope tried not to panic as she continued her descent. If she was standing there, would she be easy to hit?

Hope could feel the grass racing through her left hand and the concrete of the wall as she fell, skinning her right hand. Her boots were scuffing up as she tried to slow her descent.

And then the ledge hit her. She fell backwards onto her bottom and rolled. Hope threw down both hands, grasping for tufts of grass. She felt her back disappear over into thin air just as she halted her descent.

Hope pulled herself back from the edge and looked up. McNeil was staring down at her.

'Nowhere to go,' he said. 'Nowhere left.'

Hope looked over the edge of the small grassy platform she was on. Halfway down the dam, water emerged. It poured into a small river. However, she wasn't sure how deep it was. The water coming out was not insignificant, although massively different from if the dam wasn't there. But what it had going for it was there seemed to be a decent flow. Could she jump to there? She tried to calculate the height.

Hope had been an excellent swimmer, although it was a while now since she'd swam. But coming with swimming was diving. Back when she was younger, she was known to dive. But this dive was not an easy one.

There was a shout from across the dam.

'Inspector.' It was Perry's voice. 'Inspector.' A shot rang out towards Perry.

'Get back,' she shouted. 'He's armed. I have the detonator,' she shouted, waving it at him.

Perry gave a thumbs up signal, which seemed completely inappropriate to the extreme situation they were in.

'We'll get you,' shouted a voice. Hope recognised Macleod. However, Ian McNeil was making his way off the dam to come down towards Hope. It might only take him a few minutes to get down to her, or at least within decent shooting range. Although he'd probably want to come all the way down. She had the detonator, after all. If he shot her, that trigger could disappear over the edge. He might never get it. So, she presumed he would come the whole way. Hope would have two or three minutes to decide what to do.

Macleod and Perry couldn't rescue her. After all, the man was armed. Macleod and Perry would never be armed. If they pretended they were, they'd just end up getting themselves killed. But Hope had a bargaining chip.

'You don't have to do this,' said Hope, thinking it was possibly the worst opening line she'd ever given. After all, didn't all the great films end that way?

'What are you on about?' said McNeil, 'of course I do. They have to understand. They have to be taught a lesson, to be instructed that they can't be like this with people.'

'But it will kill you, and it will kill me,' said Hope. 'And I can't let you do that.'

'Looks like you're running out of choices, Detective Inspector. I'll let you climb back up though, get on to the hill. I don't want to kill you. I don't want you to suffer, but if you stop me, you will. Understand that it's nothing personal, but you will.'

Hope turned and stared at the drop beyond her. She'd have to fling herself. The arms would have to go wide. It would be a long way down. She undid her belt and instead used it to go round her wrist. Between the belt and her wrist, Hope attached the detonator, carefully wrapping the belt, so it didn't sit on top of the buttons.

Tying it to herself meant there was no going back. As Hope saw it, she had two choices. Stay there and end up getting shot, or stay there, hand over the device, and go up the mountainside. But that wasn't an option. She was a police officer. An officer wouldn't let people die without a fight. Or she could risk it all.

She looked back up, but McNeil was now halfway down. The gun was still in his hand but he was front facing the dam as he slid down as Hope had done. To get the gun off him, in this tight space, would be nigh impossible.

He wouldn't come onto the platform; he would be too close. He'd stop himself, and he'd turn round. In truth, she was amazed how he worked his prosthetic. She wasn't sure where the join was on the leg, or how much independent control he had over it but he seemed to more than get by with it.

Hope thought about John. Thought about the family they wanted. *If I get out of here, that's what we'll do, and nothing's going to stop me. Nothing at all. If I have to give up the force for our family, I'll do it. If I have to get at them to make things work, I'll do it.*

'My John,' she said out loud. Hope turned and looked one more time at the river below.

'I'm practically there,' said MacNeil. 'Don't make me do this. I don't want to shoot you. I get it. You're doing your job. You've done it well, better than most. You shouldn't die for that. You shouldn't die because you were the clever one.'

'If I was that clever, I'd have brought a gun,' said Hope. She laughed, but it was weak. A parrying tactic, a way to keep him occupied for a few seconds more.

'Your friends over there, they'll miss you. You shouldn't do this. After all, you've probably got somebody to go home to, haven't you?'

'John's my partner,' said Hope. 'But he knows what I am. A police officer, first and foremost. Anyone that knows me knows that.'

'You're the one off the telly, aren't you?' the man said.

Hope was a little taken aback by the statement. At a time like this, it seemed strange to bring it up.

'Yes I am,' she said.

'Is that him up there? Macleod?'

'It is.'

'Well, at least you've got the limelight this time,' said McNeil. He laughed hollowly. And then he said, for the last time, 'Give me the device and get out of here.'

Hope took a step in on the platform, and another one until

she was up against the edge of the dam wall.

'I can't do that,' she said. 'And I can't let you do this.'

Suddenly she turned on her heel, ran hard and jumped off the platform, arms spread wide.

Hope glided. The drop was a long one, but she did her best to hold the form, her hands spread wide and then pushed out in front of her. If it wasn't deep, if it wasn't capable of taking her plunge, at least it would end quick at this speed, her brain dashed on the rocks below. As she descended rapidly towards the water, involuntarily, she simply mouthed, 'John.'

The water came up fast.

Chapter 25

Hope McGrath walked into her office and was bemused by the poster on the right-hand side. It was long. On one side of it was pictured a sheer drop. At the bottom was some sort of hole.

Numbers had been calculated. Probabilities. Something mentioned survivability and talking about the detail of how accurate you had to be with your dive.

They had released her from the hospital the day before. John had been by her side. They were happy to let her go late in the day, and it was only John with her when she'd left the hospital. She'd gone home and then woken up at five in the morning.

Hope had made her way into the station. Of course, she should have stayed off. But having been rescued from the water, she didn't really know what had happened.

She hadn't quite gone unconscious because she remembered getting back up to the top of the water. But the flow had knocked her here and there and wherever before throwing her up onto some rocks. At that point, she thought she had hit her head. At least that's why the doctor said she was in for the observation, just to make sure that the head hadn't been damaged in any serious way.

She smiled at the poster, wondering which one of them had put it up. There was a cough from behind her.

'Seoras,' she said, spinning round. He was looking at her with a slight concern on his face.

'Do I look all right?' she said. It was black jeans this time, other boots, and another t-shirt.

'Well, you haven't lost your dress sense, have you?' said Macleod.

The little quips were coming more and more these days. She wondered if he just felt he could say whatever, being the older statesman in the station. He walked forward, threw his arms around her, and hugged her tight.

'When I saw you jump, I feared the worst,' he said. 'I knew you could swim, but it was quite some dive.'

'Needs be as needs must,' she said. 'I was just glad that the device didn't go off. I strapped it to me. Couldn't let him have it. He'd have killed all those people. It'd have been—'

'So, you sacrificed yourself. Or at least, possibly so,' said Macleod.

'You'd have done the same.'

'No,' said Macleod. 'I would have jumped, not dived. And I probably would have hit rocks on the way down. So, yes, I'd have sacrificed myself. But I'd have done it properly.'

She laughed. Her arms were sore. They'd taken quite an impact when they hit the water, even though she'd braced them correctly.

'And where is he—McNeil?' she asked.

Macleod shook his head. 'McNeil was going down with the ship. When you jumped and he saw you come out the other side, he went after you. Unfortunately, he doesn't dive like you do.'

Hope screwed her face up. 'He was a victim, you know.'

'We're all victims of something,' said Macleod. 'Doesn't mean you have to choose to—'

'No, it doesn't,' said Hope. 'I wasn't saying that. But how those builders—'

'Those builders are going to have major issues. They've been skirting major issues for most of their existence, in whatever business they were. But you did good.'

'I'm not sure Jim will see it that way,' said Hope nervously.

'Jim came to see me yesterday. Let's say that Jim and I fell out.'

'He didn't see I was right then.'

'Of course, he saw you were right,' said Macleod. 'Because you were right. But you disrespected him in front of everyone. That's how he sees it.'

'You always said it wasn't about that, the rank, whatever; it was about the people.'

'I still say it,' said Macleod. 'Completely. But I've annoyed enough seniors above me in my lifetime.'

'Where is everyone, anyway?' asked Hope.

'They'll be in about ten. I told them not to come in early. They're okay. A lot better now you're okay.'

'Who gives them ten o'clock?' said Holt with a grin.

'Generous DCI,' said Macleod with a straight face. 'They deserved it. They had a shock. Susan will not be right though.'

'She's struggling.'

'Big time. And what this has done, seeing a man who had a similar thing happen to him, and where he's gone, it's made her question things. The good side to that is she's facing up to what's happened, and she's going to get counselling. She'll be all right in the end, I think. Well, I pray.'

'So, what does it mean for her job?'

'Well, I wanted her to take three months off,' said Macleod. 'I was going to insist, but something's come up that I can put her to. Shouldn't give her a lot of hassle. It'll allow her to work without being around people who knew her before. People who look at her as if they're questioning whether or not she's going to be okay. Is she coping? It'll put some distance between Perry and her as well.'

'Is he all right?'

'He's not, you know,' said Macleod. 'I think he needs to be away from Susan for a bit. You get to that stage in life and Perry hasn't got anyone. He felt quite attracted to her. I'm hoping a bit of distance will keep them honest about where they are.'

'You sound like an agony aunt,' said Hope.

'Touchy, feely—that's what they say about me,' said Macleod. Hope raised her eyebrows. 'On the bright side,' he continued, 'Ross will be okay. He's just had to learn that he needs to balance home and work. The key thing, I guess, is home's the most important thing.'

'On that front,' said Hope, 'there's going to be some changes coming with me.'

'It's your life. It's your job. Don't let it swallow you up the way it swallowed me. Until you, and then especially until Jane, came at me, it was a place I hid. I know you're not hiding. But let it just be a workplace. Be Hope, not DI McGrath. That's the most important thing,' said Macleod.

'How many people know about what I just did?' said Hope.

'Well, Perry. Those who pulled you out of the river and took you off in the ambulance. Jim.'

'It's not public knowledge then,' said Hope.

'No,' said Macleod, 'it's not. It will be by ten-thirty.'

'What do you mean?'

'Press conference. I'm taking it. I'm going to tell them what you did.'

'No. You don't need to do that, Seoras.'

'I do. The papers have got your dissension front and centre. They don't know what happened up there. Jim isn't a bad man. But they don't like it when you do that to them. They were just going to keep it quiet. Let it happen. I'm going to explain exactly what you did. That it was all you.'

'I don't need that, Seoras. I'm not that vain. You never broadcast what you did.'

'No, because I'm not that vain either,' he said. 'However, they don't get to do that to you. They don't get to have your name rubbished to maintain their image. I'm going to do this because it's going to give you some kudos amongst the station, amongst all the staff. They like you already. But I am sick of you being my shadow. I'm sick of you going to places and people say, oh you're the one with Macleod. You're Hope. You're the copper-top inspector, or whatever they want to call you these days.'

'The good-looking one,' said Hope.

He laughed. 'You deserve this. And if they give you a medal for it, or they give you an award ceremony, or get you introduced to the mayor, you go and you do it. You owe it to every other decent officer out there who would do what you did. And you owe it to stick two fingers up to the old boys' network. They got it wrong. They didn't trust you.'

'You did,' said Hope.

'I've always trusted you. I've always trusted you would come through. You needed a bit of help here and there. You needed to change your way of thinking at times. But on this one, you did,' said Macleod, pointing to his head. 'Up there. You didn't grind this one out. You had to put two and two together and get a hundred. And yes, you checked with Perry. And Perry clocked it in about two minutes, flat. But you did it. You went off piste. You didn't just hammer through the way you do. You did well, Hope. I fear I'm sounding like a doting father. But you did really well.'

'I'll get you a coffee,' said Hope.

'You can. In fact, why don't we go out to breakfast? You and me. But you need to do one thing first.'

'What?'

'Come with me.'

Macleod led the way up the stairs, onto the upper floor. He walked past his office, and went further round.

'Oh no. You don't need to do this.'

'Do what?' asked Macleod.

'You don't need to haul me in front of Jim and take him down a peg for me.'

'I'm not taking him down a peg. You are,' said Macleod. 'He didn't come to the hospital. So worried were they about their image, they let that story go in the paper. You go in there and you vent. You go in there and you put him in his place. Don't lose control. Be accurate. Be devastating.'

'It's not me though, is it?'

'Oh yes, it is. But you don't do it. You play by the book. I'm the DI. He's the ACC. Therefore, I don't give him that sort of lip. You're in the big school now, Hope. You've got to fight for everything. And if they do that to you, you kick back.'

He turned and looked at her. 'Do me proud,' he said. Macleod knocked on the door, then turned and walked past

Hope. 'I'll be in my office. Don't be too long. I'm starving.'

'Come in,' said Jim from inside the office.

Hope put her hand on the door handle. She glanced back down the corridor, seeing Macleod disappearing. *Own it, be it,* she thought to herself. She pushed the door open.

'I need a word with you, if you don't mind, Jim,' said Hope.

She closed the door behind her. Her heart was thumping. But the words were ringing in her head. Be accurate. Be devastating. And she'd tell Macleod all about it over breakfast.

Read on to discover the Patrick Smythe series!

THE
WOMAN ON
THE MARINA
A PATRICK SMYTHE
MYSTERY THRILLER
G R JORDAN

Patrick Smythe is a former Northern Irish policeman who after suffering an amputation after a bomb blast, takes to the sea between the west coast of Scotland and his homeland to ply his trade as a private investigator. Join Paddy as he tries to work to his own ethics while knowing how to bend the rules he once enforced. Working from his beloved motorboat 'Craigantlet', Paddy decides to rescue a drug mule in this short story from the pen of G R Jordan.

Join G R Jordan's monthly newsletter about forthcoming releases and special writings for his tribe of avid readers and then receive your free Patrick Smythe short story.

Go to https://bit.ly/PatrickSmythe for your Patrick Smythe journey to start!

About the Author

GR Jordan is a self-published author who finally decided at forty that in order to have an enjoyable lifestyle, his creative beast within would have to be unleashed. His books mirror that conflict in life where acts of decency contend with self-promotion, goodness stares in horror at evil, and kindness blindsides us when we at our worst. Corrupting our world with his parade of wondrous and horrific characters, he highlights everyday tensions with fresh eyes whilst taking his methodical, intelligent mainstays on a roller-coaster ride of dilemmas, all the while suffering the banter of their provocative sidekicks.

A graduate of Loughborough University where he masqueraded as a chemical engineer but ultimately played American football, Gary had worked at changing the shape of cereal flakes and pulled a pallet truck for a living. Watching vegetables freeze at -40'C was another career highlight and he was also one of the Scottish Highlands "blind" air traffic controllers.

These days he has graduated to answering a telephone to people in trouble before telephoning other people to sort it out.

Having flirted with most places in the UK, he is now based in the Isle of Lewis in Scotland where his free time is spent between raising a young family with his wife, writing, figuring out how to work a loom and caring for a small flock of chickens. Luckily, his writing is influenced by his varied work and life experience as the chickens have not been the poetical inspiration he had hoped for!

You can connect with me on:

https://grjordan.com

https://facebook.com/carpetlessleprechaun

Subscribe to my newsletter:

https://bit.ly/PatrickSmythe

Also by G R Jordan

G R Jordan writes across multiple genres including crime, dark and action adventure fantasy, feel good fantasy, mystery thriller and horror fantasy. Below is a selection of his work. Whilst all books are available across online stores, signed copies are available at his personal shop.

The Absent Sculptor (Highlands & Islands Detective Book 36)

https://grjordan.com/product/the-absent-sculptor

A renowned sculptor vanishes without a trace. His latest masterpiece found smashed to pieces. Can DI Clarissa Urquhart chisel away at the lies to reveal the ugly truth behind the artist's disappearance?

When a celebrated sculptor goes missing from his remote Highland studio, DI Clarissa Urquhart is called to investigate. As her team uncover a web of jealousy, deceit, and hidden obsessions in the art world, they race against time to find the artist before he becomes the final piece in a twisted collection. Will Clarissa's keen eye for detail unveil a masterpiece of deception, or will the case remain an unfinished work?

Amidst the dust and marble, a sculpture of intrigue unfolds!

Kirsten Stewart Thrillers

https://grjordan.com/product/a-shot-at-democracy

Join Kirsten Stewart on a shadowy ride through the underbelly of the Highlands of Scotland where among the beauty and splendour of the majestic landscape lies corruption and intrigue to match any city. From murders to extortion, missing children to criminals operating above the law, the Highland former detective must learn a tougher edge to her work as she puts her own life on the line to protect those who cannot defend themselves.

Having left her beloved murder investigation team far behind, Kirsten has to battle personal tragedy and loss while adapting to a whole new way of executing her duties where your mistakes are your own. As Kirsten comes to terms with working with the new team, she often operates as the groups solo field agent, placing herself in danger and trouble to rescue those caught on the dark side of life. With action packed scenes and tense scenarios of murder and greed, the Kirsten Stewart thrillers will have you turning page after page to see your favourite Scottish lass home!

There's life after Macleod, but a whole new world of death!

Jac's Revenge (A Jack Moonshine Thriller #1)

https://grjordan.com/product/jacs-revenge

An unexpected hit makes Debbie a widow. The attention of her man's killer spawns a brutal yet classy alter ego. But how far can you play the game before it takes over your life?

All her life, Debbie Parlor lived in her man's shadow, knowing his work was never truly honest. She turned her head from news stories and rumours. But when he was disposed of for his smile to placate a rival crime lord, Jac Moonshine was born. And when Debbie is paid compensation for her loss like her car was written off, Jac decides that enough is enough.

Get on board with this tongue-in-cheek revenge thriller that will make you question how far you would go to avenge a loved one, and how much you would enjoy it!

A Giant Killing (Siobhan Duffy Mysteries #1)
https://grjordan.com/product/a-giant-killing
A body lies on the Giant's boot. Discord, as the master of secrets has been found. Can former spy Siobhan Duffy find the killer before they execute her former colleagues?

When retired operative Siobhan Duffy sees the killing of her former master in the paper, her unease sends her down a path of discovery and fear. Aided by her young housekeeper and scruff of a gardener, Siobhan begins a quest to discover the reason for her spy boss' death and unravels a can of worms today's masters would rather keep closed. But in a world of secrets, the difference between revenge and simple, if brutal, housekeeping becomes the hardest truth to know.

The past is a child who never leaves home!

Milton Keynes UK
Ingram Content Group UK Ltd.
UKHW041628240924
448733UK00002B/35

9 781915 562975